BAD PENGUIN

BAD PENGUIN

A very dangerous movie!

A screenplay by
Phil Clarke Jr.

First Printing 2019

ISBN 978-0-578-11347-0

A **DRAWASSIC** book
www.drawastic.com

Why did DRAWASSIC decide to publish a series of animated movie scripts that I have never made? Simple because, having struggled for a lifetime to get support for my filmmaking visions and meeting nothing but apathy and disinterest from the industry, I at least wanted to the public to have a chance to see what I say, to share a vision of animated filmmaking that is different to the mainstream and yet – I believe – has a valid voice in the world of entertainment filmmaking. The scripts published in this series are not all written by me but are certainly molded by what I was trying to achieve with animation – and they are certainly very different in style and approach. Once upon a time, when a certain Walt Disney has a unique vision and animation was pushed further and further towards imaginative storytelling and groundbreaking visual originality there was a chance to go beyond the formulaic and the predictable. Now all that has changed of course and despite my having made over 200 TV commercials (many award-winning), two TV Specials, several Short Films (one of which winning a BAFTA) and the title sequence for "The Pink Panther Strikes Again" movie, I have never been given a chance to show what I can do with a full-length movie venture – either in the mainstream or indie worlds. It is not as if my ideas were to out there and strange for modern audiences. Indeed, I challenge readers to deny that when reading the scripts I am publishing in this series of books. It's more the fact that the industry today has preconceived ideas of what audiences what, applying formulas of design, storytelling and subject matter that the industry, in its infinite wisdom, deems worthy of laying before modern audiences. It doesn't help too that with the advent of technology and the digital revolution the old-school notion of hand-drawn animation is no longer fashionable, unless of course is can be compromised and fashioned into what is deemed formulaic enough for the industry norms. I hope therefore in publishing these scripts readers will be able to make their own minds up on what is appealing to animation audiences and what is not. Remember however that all of these scripts are *"first-draft"* screenplays and have yet to go through the production mill that will enable many minds and many artistic

talents to form them into what might be an amazing animated experience. Nevertheless, I feel confident that the subject matter of each script will speak for itself and hint at what might have been, were there a little more vision, imagination and creative bravery in the industry they were designed for.

I thank you for giving this script a fair hearing in the court of public opinion!

Sincerely,

Tony White.

Concept Art introduction:

A great deal of initial development has been created for "Bad Penguin", in addition to an animated teaser to be found here... http://www.badpenguinmovie.com.

The truth is however that we still have a long way to go to arrive at the kind of sharp, sophisticated, comic book style of graphic imagery that will make this film as unique and groundbreaking as we envision it to be. In the meantime the following pages should provide a hint of the ground covered so far....

We also offer a huge thanks to all those talented artists who have contributed to this project thus far *(listed in alphabetical order)*...

Heather Gross

Neil Hanson

Thomas Liera

Peter Moehrle

Tara Mueller

Sergey Naygel

Gerritt Perkins

Rune Rennicke

Dominic Sodano

Dean Yeagle

...and of course anyone else we may have forgotten!

Concept Art: EARLY PENGUIN DESIGN

Concept Art: EARLY PENGUIN DESIGN

Concept Art: EARLY "COOPER" SKETCH

Concept Art: FINAL "BAD PENGUIN" MODEL SHEET

Concept Art: FINAL "COOPER" DESIGNS

Concept Art: EARLY PROMOTIONAL PIECES

Concept Art: EARLY LAYOUT VISUAL

"Tis the season to be grouchy!"

Concept Art: EARLY PROMOTIONAL PIECES

Concept Art: EARLY PROMOTIONAL PIECES

Concept Art: EARLY LAYOUT THUMBNAILS

Concept Art: PENCIL TEST FRAME & ANIMATION LAYOUT

Concept Art: ORIGINAL TEASER STORYBOARD

Director's introduction:

"Bad Penguin" is a mile away from my normal style of animation!

In truth my reputation has been born of producing high quality work for a family style audience ~ a thing that's mainly the result of a long and successful career in producing TV commercials and other inspirationally minded films. Therefore when Phil Clarke Jr.'s wife, Janet, first approached me with the script I found myself somewhat uncomfortable when reading the opening violent scenes that introduce the obnoxious, crazy bird to the world. As I read on however I started to be captivated with everything I was reading.

I was actually on a road trip at the time and found myself incredibly impatient for our next stop, so I could get back to the script and read the next pages. In the end I forced myself to stop driving until I could finish the entire script, contact Janet and declare my total commitment to the project! In some inexplicable way the "Penguin" had captured my heart, as objectionable and disgusting a character as he really is!

In truth, I think it was actually the warm, elderly, man-of-color, jazz musician, "Cooper" – seeming foil and confidant to the Penguin – who really captured my heart. Without risking a spoiler for the script you're about to read I think his role in the whole affair is both heart warming and redeeming. I find I can get past the nasty and violent nature of the Penguin, simply because I know that ultimately Cooper's compassion, wisdom and unconditional love for the wild bird will ultimately win out – or at least that was my hope was I ferociously read the script for that very first time. How in heaven's name Cooper can see any redeeming qualities in the Bad Penguin in the first place is beyond me? But he does and that is what makes this story so wonderfully balanced in my imagination.

So, for those of you of a more prudish nature ~ as I was, pre-Penguin ~ who also may find the initial impact of this story offensive, or at least challenging, I urge you to read on as there is something quite magical and ultimately inspiring with this script. Like the alchemists of old, who allegedly turned crude lead into pure gold, author Phil Clarke Jr. has conjured up here a dark and murky world here that ultimately shines light onto our human condition.

For this reason alone I hope you will give the script of "Bad Penguin" more than just a passing look, and hope also that you can envision the tremendous potential I see in this unique film as a mature animation classic. As one who finds previous X-rated animated films significantly trivial, poorly executed and quite simply awful, I trust

you can imagine this one as an amazing piece of storytelling mastery ~ albeit it that it is set in a world that I think none of us would choose to venture into if the opportunity ever presented itself!

I welcome you to the dark side of light!

Tony White
www.tonywhiteanimation.com

Author's introduction:

"What a Fowl Waterfowl!

The creation of Bad Penguin was actually an accident; a convergence of bizarre visuals and themes that somehow… clicked just right.

My wife wanted to learn how to use scriptwriting software. How better to teach her than writing a quick n' dirty short? Ten minutes and truck-loads of derangement later, a two page bloody and chaotic tale emerged: about a rogue penguin who attacks an unsuspecting victim in a playground… with a cocktail fork?!?

I posted this instant "classic" to a scriptwriting board I haunted at the time. Those who read it were fascinated - though they couldn't explain why. It made no fucking sense, but several begged for more. Three other shorts followed, revolving around irreverent plots - each more unhinged than the last (including the Penguin wrecking a grocery store, scheming to score a date in an abortion clinic, or showing how far he'd go to get a beak's-full of scotch.) Shockingly, the Penguin's growing fan-base ate it up. Which meant…

I had to write a feature. But I aspired to much more than just a hundred pages of some cuckoo bird wreaking random acts of insanity. No, Bad Penguin needed to STAND for something on his not-so-happy feet. And thus he evolved into an anti-hero. One with a heart of feathered gold, who did "attempt" to accomplish good in this world – albeit in a wildly destructive way.

In what crazy world could this occur? Though many penguins choose nature for their outdoorsy crib, *this* Penguin informed me he felt at home with urban film noir - trapped between the grimy walls of fictional Clover City; a hood populated by guns, violence, dames, and an array of down-trodden denizens who have since forgotten how to care.

Except for one shining exception: a blind street musician named Cooper. As months flew by, the feature practically wrote itself. Cooper emerged as the Yin to Bad Penguin's Yang. The Penguin's only friend, proved himself the only character capable of soothing the pain raging in the Penguin's tiny heart.

Speaking of "tiny": Bad Penguin may have originated as a goof… but he's waddled a long, long way out of Antarctica since then. His story's grown, too. No longer a short

written for shock value and Quentin Tarantino giggles, Bad Penguin incorporates universal human, heart felt themes: the power of friendship. Redemption. Greek Tragedy.

No matter what you get from this animated read, one thing's certain. He may have hatched as just a misunderstood Bad Penguin, but this unique tale's flapping its wings, ready to fly!

Phil Clarke Jr.
www.philclarkejr.com

FADE IN:

EXT. CLOVER CITY - NIGHT

Snow falls over the metropolis. Dirigibles float overhead.

Two intersecting highways divide the city. Connecting loops form a cloverleaf, illuminated by headlights.

A lone saxophone plays Christmas music.

                    COOPER (V.O.)
          In the months following the end of World
          War 2, Clover City prospered.

EXT. STREET - CONTINUOUS

Snow coats the street, decorated for Christmas. Well-dressed SHOPPERS bustle along, wrapped boxes and bags in their hands.

A WEALTHY-LOOKING OBESE WOMAN (40) leaves the department store, wearing a mink coat and fancy hat. She pets the Pomeranian in her hands... the most precious thing in her life.

                    COOPER (V.O.)
          From the wealthiest of the wealthy...

A uniformed chauffer helps the woman into a limousine as a NANNY (25) juggles a swaddling baby and several large department store bags.

COOPER (60), a thin black man stands on the sidewalk. He plays a lively Christmas tune saxophone. He wears dark glasses and layers of old clothes.

                    COOPER (V.O.)
          To the poorest of the poor--

A passerby drops some change in Cooper's sax case. Cooper smiles. Doesn't miss a beat.

                    COOPER (V.O.)
          Like me.

A Salvation Army SANTA RINGS his bell.

                    COOPER (V.O.)
          With our boys back home, the demand for
          consumer goods increased.

Store windows display television sets, radios and toys.

COOPER (V.O.)
And with the demand, came the need to
produce them.

INT. DEPARTMENT STORE - CONTINUOUS

Cheerful CLERKS ring up sales in the crowded store.

COOPER (V.O.)
Everyone was working. Everyone was
happy.

A young GIRL (8) sits on SANTA's lap. Other KIDS stand in line, anxiously
wait their turn.

COOPER (V.O.)
Things were darned near perfect....

An air vent overlooks the scene. BRIGHT YELLOW EYES with RED PUPILS
stare through metal slants.

COOPER (V.O.)
Until HE showed up.

The vent cover explodes off the walls, hitting an artificial Christmas tree.
Bulbs POP. The cover SLAMS to the floor.

A MACARONI PENGUIN leaps from the vent. His trench coat opens like a
cape. He somersaults in the air, spraying bullets from semi-automatic pistols.

PEOPLE SCREAM.

The Penguin lands near Santa. The fat man and little girl stare at him.

The Penguin stares back with hate-filled eyes. His feathered uni-brow is
crossed by a bright red scar.

Magazines drop from the pistols. He slaps in fresh mags--

CLICK-CLICK!

And aims at Santa.

COOPER (V.O.)
"Hello Santa... I never got the pony I
always wanted," he told the department
store Santa.

The store falls quiet. Music plays over the intercom.

COOPER (V.O.)
"Every year, I asked for a pony and you
never got me one. And I've been good.
So good it hurt."

A MAN steps over the velvet ropes, behind the Penguin, and tiptoes forward.

COOPER (V.O.)
"Now you'll learn the pain I went
through."

The man edges closer.

Without looking, the Penguin swings a wing back--

BLAM!

--and shoots him in the knee. The man goes down SCREAMING.

COOPER (V.O.)
"You all will."

He steps toward Santa. The little girl SOBS in her mittens.

COOPER (V.O.)
"But I'll give you a chance to save your
life."

He aims his guns at Santa's chest.

COOPER (V.O.)
"I'll count to ten," he said. "Then I'm
going to shoot."

Sweat pours from Santa's face.

COOPER (V.O.)
"You want to save your miserable life?
Use the girl."

People GASP.

COOPER (V.O.)
"One... Two..."

Parents hug their horrified children.

COOPER (V.O.)
"Three... Four..."

Santa and the girl look at each other.

                    SANTA
          But I'm not Santa--

                    COOPER (V.O.)
          "Five... Six..."

The girl CRIES some more.

                    SANTA
          I'm just a store employee--

                    COOPER (V.O.)
          "Seven... Eight..."

A woman faints. Her presents CLATTER on the floor.

                    COOPER (V.O.)
          "Nine..."

Santa lifts the girl and holds her in front of him.

                    COOPER (V.O.)
          "Ten!"

The Penguin swings his guns, attempts to get a bead on the man. Urine rolls
down the girl's leg, onto the floor.

                    SHOPPER (V.O.)
                  (whisper)
          He's sacrificing the girl...

The Penguin continues his attempt to get a clear shot.

                    COOPER (V.O.)
          "I got a present for you, kid," he told the
          girl. "One you'll keep the rest of your life...
          Reality!"

The Penguin leaps onto the back of Santa's chair. He springs atop Santa's
workshop. Dives into the vent and disappears.

The crowd glares at Santa. He sinks slowly in his chair, still clutching the
SCREAMING girl like a life vest.

EXT. STREET - MINUTES LATER

The Penguin races from the store.

He hits an icy patch and gracefully circles a woman carrying wrapped boxes with bows.

She spins around with him and SCREAMS. Gifts fly everywhere. The Penguin races down the street.

> COOPER (V.O.)
> It's amazing how much ruckus one
> flightless bird can cause.

The Penguin races past Cooper.

The musician stops playing and listens as webbed feet pass him by. He shakes his head. Returns to his music.

EXT. DEERBORN STREET - LATER

A run down neighborhood. Apartment windows are boarded up, garbage piled high.

> COOPER (V.O.)
> No one knew where he came from. Or
> why he was here. Or why he hated
> Christmas so much.

The DEERBORN TAVERN squats in the middle of the street. People huddle around a burning garbage can.

INT. DEERBORN TAVERN - CONTINUOUS

The bar is old and in need of repair. Much like the patrons. Undesirables sit in the smoked-filled bar.

TINNY CHRISTMAS MUSIC plays on the radio.

> COOPER (V.O.)
> Hell, no one knows if there was a reason
> for any of this.

Cooper sits at the end of the bar, beer in his hand. His sax case leans against the wall.

> COOPER (V.O.)
> All anyone knew was that he was here.

The Penguin sits next to him. He gulps down a shot and stacks the glass in a pyramid of other glasses. He chases the shot with a beer.

                    COOPER
          You know, that stunt you pulled cost me
          money, today.

The Penguin peers at him from the corner of his eye.

                    COOPER
          Police cars showed up. Ambulances. I
          think even a fire truck did. You set the
          place on fire or something?

The Penguin CHUCKLES.

                    COOPER
          They cleared the street. Told everyone to
          move on.

Behind the bar, MICKEY (60) pries open the lid on an antique sandwich
maker. A cigarette dangles from his mouth.

He flips a grilled cheese sandwich onto a plate.

                    COOPER
          You know I make most of my money this
          time of year, right?

Mickey slides the plate in front of OZZIE, a sad-looking man.

                    OZZIE
          Thanks, Mickey.

                    COOPER (O.C.)
          People are nice to the poor blind colored
          man playing Christmas songs on his sax.
          You know that, right?

The penguin reaches into his (invisible) pocket and pulls out cash. He peels
off ten and places it in front of Cooper.

The money FLAPS on the bar.

Cooper stops drinking.

                    COOPER
          Did you just put money down in front of
          me? Did you?

He turns to the Penguin.

                    COOPER

I don't need your charity. I work for a
living.

The Penguin looks at him, a little peeved.

                    COOPER
          I get paid to play my saxophone.

The two stare at each other. People in the bar watch them.

                    COOPER
          Nobody ever wins a staring contest with a
          blind man. Not you. Not nobody. Put it
          away.

Cooper slides the ten back over to the Penguin.

                    COOPER
          You wanna give your money away, buy
          the people here a drink. Or a cheese
          sandwich.

The Penguin looks at RUDY (65) on his other side. Dressed in shabby clothes,
the man flashes a pitiful grin.

The Penguin gives him 'the finger.' Rudy's smile disappears.

Cooper swirls his near empty glass.

                    MICKEY
          Need another one, Cooper?

                    COOPER
          Why not, Mickey. And one for my friend
          as well.

Mickey grabs a glass and pours.

                    MICKEY
          Did you hear that Gina-Lee is back?

                    COOPER
          Gina-Lee? Thought she married that club
          owner and left Candletown.

                    MICKEY
          Wasn't no club owner. Just a piano
          player, married to two other girls. Fool
          couldn't afford to keep one wife, much
          less three.

                    COOPER
          That poor girl.

                    MICKEY
                 (to Penguin)
          Screaming Turkey?

The Penguin holds up two 'fingers.'

                    MICKEY
          Double? You got it.

He grabs a bottle from behind the bar.

                    MICKEY
          Gina-Lee's brother catches that fool,
          won't be nothing left of him--

                    CHINNY (O.S.)
          Hey, Wee Billy! I thought we was in a bar!

CHINNY MONROE and WEE BILLY JEFFERSON (30s) stand at the doorway.
Slick-looking black hustlers with expensive zoot suits and "we're here to
start trouble" grins.

Chinny towers over the diminutive Wee Billy by a foot.

                    WEE BILLY
          Yeah, Chinny! I thought we was in a bar,
          too.

They strut in.

                    CHINNY
          But this is like a funeral home.

                    WEE BILLY
                 (guffaws)
          Funeral home! This place is exactly like a
          funeral home!

Patrons hide their faces and shrink in their chairs.

                    WEE BILLY
          I remember my gran'mama's funeral and
          it was--!

Chinny puts his hand on Wee Billy's chest.

                    CHINNY

We don't need to know about your dead
gran'mama.

Wee Billy looks hurt. Chinny steps to the bar.

                    CHINNY
          This is Christmas. A time for giving.
          Celebrating--

                    MICKEY
          What the hell you two fools got to
          celebrate?

He gives the Penguin his drink. The Penguin watches Chinny and Wee Billy
suspiciously.

                    MICKEY
          Who gives you the right to come in here in
          them fool suits?

                    CHINNY
          Who gives us the right?

He reaches into his breast pocket...

                    CHINNY
          President Jackson gives us the right!

And SLAPS a twenty on the bar.

                    WEE BILLY
             (guffaws)
          President Jackson! 'Cause he's on the ten
          dollar bill!

                    CHINNY
          He's on the twenty, you fool!
             (to Mickey)
          Wee Billy and I are successful
          businessmen who believe in sharing the
          wealth. The drinks are on us!

SUBDUED CHEERING rises from the PATRONS not passed out.

                    MICKEY
          I ain't taking your money!

Mickey throws the money at Chinny. The CHEERING abruptly ends. Wee
Billy struggles to catch the fluttering bill before it hits the floor.

                    MICKEY

It's dirty.

                    CHINNY
          Dirty?

Wee Billy examines the bill with a confused look.

                    MICKEY
          You don't think I know where that money
          comes from? Hell, we all know! You
          selling 'H.' In our neighborhood. Both of
          you!

                    CHINNY
          We provide a product. We don't force
          nobody to buy it!

Mickey leans over the bar, in Chinny's face.

                    MICKEY
          You sell death! And I don't want it here.
          Now get out 'fore I throw you out!

                    CHINNY
          Throw me out? You and what army?

The Penguin draws a switchblade--

SNICK!

Light glistens off the blade.

                    COOPER
          Put it away.

The Penguin looks at him. Cooper faces straight ahead.

                    COOPER
          I said, 'put it away.'

The Penguin slowly lowers the knife.

GUNNER (40) rises from his stool. He's huge, big enough to rip a man's head
off. Two medals hang on his army jacket.

His right arm is missing; his jacket sleeve is rolled up and pinned to his side.

                    GUNNER
                (to Chinny)
          If Mickey says you gots to go, then you
          gots to go.

ROBERTS (30) gets up. He's an obese man wearing an army coat that no longer fits.

> ROBERTS
> Gunner's right. You gots to go.

Roberts walks over. The floor GROANS with each step.

Chinny and Wee Billy exchange nervous looks. Chinny forces an insincere smile.

> CHINNY
> Hey, let's all be cool. We just came in to
> spread some Christmas--

> GUNNER
> If Mickey says you gots to go--

> ROBERTS
> Then you gots to go!

Gunner and Roberts herd Chinny and Wee Billy to the door.

> CHINNY
> Okay. Okay. No need to get crazy.

Wee Billy and Chinny are tossed out. The door closes with a noticeable SCRAPE.

> MICKEY
> Beers and grilled cheese sandwiches are
> on me!

Everyone in the bar CHEERS.

> MICKEY
> For these two, you lazy-assed fools.

The CHEERS fade to GRUMBLING. Gunner and Robert pat each other on the back and return to their stools.

The Penguin SIGHS.

> COOPER
> See? We been looking after our own, long
> before you showed up.

Mickey tosses cheese sandwiches into his sandwich machine.

> MICKEY

You want another one, Coop?

                    COOPER
          Just the bill, Mickey. What's the damage?

Mickey steps up to him.

                    MICKEY
          Let's see. Two-forty.

                    COOPER
          Two-forty? Your prices going up?

                    MICKEY
          No. Just how much you two are drinking.

The two CHUCKLE. Cooper counts off two bills and change.

He grabs his saxophone and cane.

                    COOPER
          Night, Mickey.

                    MICKEY
          Night, Coop.

Cooper makes his way through the bar.

                    GUNNER
          Good night, Cooper.

                    ROBERTS
          Get home safe.

                    COOPER
          Good night, boys.

He walks out the door. The bar goes quiet as a tomb.

The Penguin lifts his drink to his mouth and looks around.

GEORGINA (40) sits at the far end of the bar, a drink in her hand and
cigarette in her mouth. She wears a slinky dress and more make up than a
circus clown.

An old man slumps next to her on the bar.

The Penguin smiles.

She looks at him, swirls her drink with her finger. Slowly places her finger in
her mouth.

The Penguin hops off his stool and disappears.

The man next to Georgina is jerked off his stool--

THUD!

The Penguin climbs up, smiling. She smiles back.

>   GEORGINA
>   (slurred)
>   I love a man in a tuxedo...

She leans against him and PURRS.

EXT. RUN-DOWN RESIDENTIAL STREET - DAY

The street is lined with old apartment buildings. Tattered curtains flap from broken windows.

INT. GEORGINA'S BEDROOM - CONTINUOUS

An accordion radiator HISSES steam, discoloring the adjacent wall. The furniture is old and mismatched.

Georgina lays in her bed, SNORING. An old blanket is pulled up to her chin.

The clock reads 7:45.

The Penguin steps from the bathroom, a towel wrapped around his waist. He looks at Georgina.

Her hair is messy. Her makeup smeared. She looks older.

The Penguin frowns.

Her legs stick out from the blanket. They're hairy with varicose veins. She's missing two toes on one foot! WTF?

A horrified look flashes on the Penguin's face.

'Damn. I slept with that?'

Georgina rolls over, exposing her privates.

The Penguin grabs his towel and wipes his tongue with it.

He heads toward the door, still using the towel. He takes one last look and SHUDDERS.

EXT. RUN-DOWN RESIDENTIAL STREET - MINUTES LATER

The Penguin steps from Georgina's apartment building, still cleaning his tongue on his flippers.

EXT. CLOVER PARK ENTRANCE - LATER

An archway towers over the entrance, flanked by a three foot stone wall.

A large pine tree is surrounded by scaffolding. Work crews string Christmas lights along the branches.

A nearby sign reads: CLOVER CITY TREE LIGHTING FRIDAY 7:00.

Cooper stands on a grating by the entrance. He plays Christmas tunes on his saxophone.

THREE KIDS eye Cooper, dirty snowballs in their hands.

                    KID 1
          You sure we should be doing this?

                    KID 2
          It'll be funny. Don't chicken out.

Kid 2 packs his snowball tightly in his hands.

                    KID 1
          Yeah, but the guy is blind. He can't even
          see.

                    KID 3
          Yeah. That means he can't point us out to
          the cops.

A WHISTLE distracts them. They look to the side.

The Penguin stands next to a THREE TIER SNOWMAN. The snowman has a carrot and coal for a face and wears a top hat.

The Penguin shakes his head at the kids.

                    KID 2
          Ehh. Just a pigeon.

Kid 2 winds up for his pitch. A basketball-sized snowball CRASHES into his face.

His friends look at the Penguin. He eats a carrot. The snowman is missing its head. The hat now rests on the torso.

The kids look at each other.

> KID 1
> You don't think...?

> KID 3
> How could he? He got no arms. Just them
> little wings.

The Penguin looks at his wings, flapping them.

> KID 3
> (whispers)
> I'm gonna do it.

Kid 3 packs his snowball tightly--

SLAM!

--he's flattened by a larger ball of snow.

Kid 1 looks at his friend. Then at the Penguin.

The Penguin leans against the bottom of the snowman, now wearing the hat. The bird SNARLS.

Kid 1 runs off. He gets about fifty feet--

CRASH!

--a snowball the size of a truck tire SLAMS down on him. His arm sticks from under the snow, twitching pitifully.

Cooper continues to play.

The Penguin belly slides on the snow up to him, wearing the top hat. He sways to the music and smiles, bewitched.

Cooper finishes. The Penguin CLAPS.

> COOPER
> That you, bird?

He SNIFFS the air in front of him.

> COOPER
> What is that smell? You been eating bad
> fish all night?

The bird looks away in shame, scrapes his tongue on his beak.

> COOPER
> Take a penny out of my case and buy
> yourself some Wrigley's, will you?

CRASH!

Cooper and the Penguin turn toward the park.

Work crews stand over an overturned box. Shards of broken glass litter the ground.

> COOPER
> Something wrong with the tree?

The Penguin GRUNTS. Cooper sits behind him on a crate.

> COOPER
> What's your beef with Christmas, bird?
> You're the only one who got a problem
> with it.

The Penguin steps to Cooper. The old man feels for his beak. The Penguin SLAPS his hand away.

> COOPER
> Had to be sure it was you. Thought I was
> talking to you yesterday. Turned out it
> was a fire hydrant.

They smile at each other. And talk (MOS).

> COOPER (V.O.)
> I asked the Penguin what it was about
> Christmas that ruffled his feathers. Didn't
> realize what I was getting into.

The muni-workers argue (MOS). Hands gesture wildly.

> COOPER (V.O.)
> The Penguin said he was tired of the lies.
> To listen to him, Christmas was all about
> lies.

A YOUNG COUPLE walks by, wearing Santa hats.

> COOPER (V.O.)
> There were lies about Santa Claus--

A muni-worker pulls a reindeer statue from a crate.

                    COOPER (V.O.)
          Lies about reindeer--

Kid 2 stirs from underneath his huge ball of snow.

                    COOPER (V.O.)
          Frosty the Snowman--

Workers unload nativity statues from a truck.

                    COOPER (V.O.)
          But when he started talking about Jesus, I
          said--

Cooper grabs the Penguin's beak.

                    COOPER
          Hold it!

The Penguin stares at him, bug-eyed.

                    COOPER
          You wanna complain about Santa Claus,
          that's one thing. But I ain't gonna let you
          badmouth Baby Jesus. I ain't!

Cooper lets him go. The Penguin blinks at him, guilt in his eyes.

                    COOPER (V.O.)
          It was the first time I ever shut him up.
          Probably the first time anyone shut him
          up.

The Penguin rants at him (MOS).

                    COOPER (V.O.)
          He told me that Christmas was about
          faith. And he had no faith in anything. If
          he couldn't see it, or feel it, then it didn't
          exist.

                    COOPER
          What about love? Does that exist?

The Penguin looks down at his feet.

                    COOPER

Or friendship? You can't say that don't exist.

The Penguin glances at Cooper with sad eyes.

EXT. RUN-DOWN RESIDENTIAL STREET - DAY

Everything's dirty.

An ELDERLY WOMAN shoves a shopping cart along the snow-covered sidewalk.

DAPHNE (25) leans against a doorway, thin and sickly. Layers of makeup cover her face. Her poorly-fitted clothing is covered in patches.

Footsteps CRUNCH in the snow.

                    DAPHNE
          Looking for a good time...?

Chinny and Wee Billy look down at her.

                    WEE BILLY
          That's what we was gonna ask you,
          Daphne.

Daphne forces a smile and fluffs her hair. Tries to look presentable.

                    CHINNY
          We been looking for you, Daphne. We're
          here to collect.

                    DAPHNE
          I tried toi find you boys earlier--

Chinny steps toward her, menacing.

                    CHINNY
          We gave you a little product on credit,
          remember? You said you'd have our
          money today.

                    DAPHNE
          Yeah, but you see--

                    CHINNY
          See? I need to see money.

                    WEE BILLY
          We need to see money, girl!

                         DAPHNE
              I been sick. Business ain't good.

                         CHINNY
              You know what else ain't good?

He shoves her against the door.

                         DAPHNE
                   Hey!

                         CHINNY
              You holding out on us ain't good!

He rifles through her pockets and pulls out several bills. He tosses the money
to Wee Billy.

                         DAPHNE
                   Wait! I need that!

                         CHINNY
              Count it, Wee Billy. How we doing?

                         WEE BILLY
              We good. With a dollar to spare.

He flamboyantly hands the single back to Daphne.

                         WEE BILLY
                   Here you go.

                         DAPHNE
              Chinny, please! Goldman's coming today.
              If I don't pay my rent, I'm sleeping on the
              street tonight.

                         CHINNY
              Well, let me help you out...

He throws her to the snow-covered sidewalk.

                         CHINNY
                   And tuck you in!

Wee Billy GUFFAWS. Daphne SCREAMS.

                         WEE BILLY
              Tuck you in! I get it! You tucked her in.
              In a bed of snow!

Chinny steps around Daphne and fixes his jacket.

                    CHINNY
          Let's get going, Wee Billy. We got
          business elsewhere.

                    WEE BILLY
          'Cause we're busy people.

The two start down the street.

                    DAPHNE (O.S.)
          Help me... please.

                    CHINNY
          Girl, ain't nobody gonna help the likes of
          you--

He and Wee Billy turn around--

The Penguin stands next to Daphne. They look at each other.

Wee Billy and Chinny look at each other.

                    WEE BILLY
          What the hell's that?

                    CHINNY
          It's a penguin, you fool. They live in the
          North Pole.

                    WEE BILLY
          Then he must be lost, 'cuz this ain't the
          North Pole.

Wee Billy pats the Penguin on the head.

The Penguin grabs his hand and throws him, martial-arts style. Wee Billy lands in a puddle with a loud--

SPLASH!

The Penguin pushes his head into the slush with a big webbed foot.

                    WEE BILLY
          gurgle

                    CHINNY
          What the hell? You think that's funny?

Chinny pulls a straight razor from a pocket--

SNICK!

And waves it menacingly.

Daphne reaches up to the Penguin.

                    DAPHNE
          Please help me...

Chinny slashes at the Penguin. The bird sidesteps.

He slashes again and again. The Penguin steps out of the way. Each time, he gets closer to his would-be attacker.

Wee Billy brushes dirty ice from his ruined suit.

                    CHINNY
              (to the Penguin)
          I'm gonna cut you like you was a
          Thanksgiving turkey--

The Penguin punches Chinny in the nose. Chinny staggers.

                    CHINNY
          Son of a bitch!

Wee Billy pulls a blackjack from a pocket. He grabs a trash can lid like a shield.

The two circle the Penguin. The bird watches warily.

                    CHINNY
          You ready Wee Billy?

                    WEE BILLY
          Oh, I'm ready. I was born ready.

                    CHINNY
          On the count of three, then. One!

The two feign attacks. Wee Billy stands with his feet far apart and his knees bent.

                    WEE BILLY
          Gonna get you for what you done to my
          suit.

                    CHINNY

Two!

                    WEE BILLY
Gonna skin you and make me a suit outta
you.

                    CHINNY
You ready for 'three,' Wee Billy?

                    WEE BILLY
Ready for a new suit!

                    CHINNY
Alright! Thr--!

The Penguin slides between Wee Billy's legs.

                    WEE BILLY
Huh?

Wee Billy looks between his legs; his tie hangs low.

The Penguin grabs his tie and yanks.

Wee Billy flips and lands on his back with a painful--

THUD!

The Penguin jumps on his stomach--

                    WEE BILLY
Oof!

--and springboards off him, soaring high in the air.

                    CHINNY
What the--?

The Penguin lands a kick to Chinny's face.

CRACK!

Chinny and the Penguin fall to the snow. The razor spins in the air, in
cartoon fashion.

The Penguin grabs it and slashes Chinny's face.

Blood mixes with dirty snow....

EXT. THE GREAT HALL - NIGHT

A ritzy restaurant with stone lions outside. The sidewalk is free of snow. Valets open limousine doors and wave well-dressed GUESTS inside.

INT. THE GREAT HALL - CONTINUOUS

Cheerful PATRONS fill the restaurant. A piano PLAYER (the only non-white) plays Christmas music with a forced smile on his face.

TERRENCE (40) pours drinks at the bar. He's thin but muscular, with bright red hair.

                    HALL (V.O.)
          When you boys told me you could handle
          Candletown, I believed you.

INT. GREGORY HALL'S OFFICE - CONTINUOUS

GREGORY HALL (55) peers at diners from a window. He's a portly man, well-dressed. His pudgy face is cold and hard.

                    HALL
          You told me you grew up there. That you
          knew everyone. I believed you then, too.

He sits behind a mahogany desk and smokes a cigar.

                    HALL
          Now you tell me you were attacked by a
          penguin.

Chinny and Wee Billy sit on the other side of the desk. Wee Billy's clothes are a mess. Chinny's face is bandaged like the Invisible Man.

                    HALL
          That this penguin stole your money. And
          the heroin I gave you.

                    WEE BILLY
          That's--that's what happened, Mister Hall.

                    CHINNY
               (slurred)
          Mister Hall. Sir. Look at my face--

                    HALL
          I'm not denying something happened.

He takes a long drag on his cigar. The room is deathly quiet as he exhales.
Chinny and Wee Billy watch the smoke curl over their heads.

                    HALL
          I just question the details.

                    WEE BILLY
          We just--

Chinny puts his hand on Wee Billy's arm and shakes his head.

                    HALL
          I read the newspapers about what
          happened in the department stores.
          About this 'bad penguin,' causing trouble
          throughout the city.

Wee Billy SIGHS in relief, smiling.

                    HALL
          I'm meeting the mayor for dinner tonight.
          I'll review the matter with him.

Chinny and Wee Billy slowly rise and head toward the door.

                    HALL
          Find out what you can and keep me
          advised.

                    WEE BILLY
          You can count on us, Mister Hall.

                    HALL
          I'm sure I can.

Chinny glances back. Hall's eyes blaze in anger.

EXT. ALLEY WAY - CONTINUOUS

Chinny and Wee Billy step onto a loading dock.

                    CHINNY
          We're in deep shit with Hall.

                    WEE BILLY
          What you mean? He seemed cool.

They shuffle down a narrow alley. Mounds of garbage lines the walls.

                    CHINNY
          He ain't cool. We gotta take care of this
          bird and get our shit back.

                    WEE BILLY
          I gotta get him back for what he done to
          my suit.

Chinny stops.

                    CHINNY
          Your suit? You're thinking about your
          suit? You stupid nigger!

He rips his bandages off. He's hideously scarred. Wee Billy looks horrified.

                    CHINNY
          That penguin scarred me for life and
          you're worried about your suit?

Chinny slaps him--

SLAP SLAP SLAP

--in the head and face. Wee Billy shields himself with his arms.

                    CHINNY
          We find this damn bird and get him back
          for what he done!

Chinny drops his hand.

                    WEE BILLY
          Get him for stealing our stuff--

Chinny raises his hand again.

                    WEE BILLY
          And your face! And your face!

Chinny storms down the alley. Wee Billy hurries after him.

                    CHINNY
          Your cousin still got them guns?

                    WEE BILLY
          G-guns?

                    CHINNY

Guns! We gotta kill that penguin. Or you
want him cutting your face up like he
done mine?

They walk from sight.

                    CHINNY (V.O.)
We do this and we take over Candletown.

                    WEE BILLY (V.O.)
          (beat)
And I can get me a new suit.

SLAP!

                    CHINNY (V.O.)
Stupid nigger.

EXT. DEERBORN TAVERN - NIGHT

Flurries cover dirty street. TINNY CHRISTMAS MUSIC floats through the air.

INT. DEERBORN TAVERN - CONTINUOUS

Cooper and the Penguin sit at one end of the bar, half-filled drinks in front of
them. Cooper holds a grilled cheese sandwich in his hand.

                    COOPER
--so the doctor says, "If this is my
thermometer, where's my pen?"

He CHUCKLES. The Penguin stares at him, blankly.

                    COOPER
"If this is my thermometer, where's my
pen?" Come on, Bird. You don't think
that's funny?

The Penguin shakes his head.

                    COOPER (V.O.)
Faith wasn't the only thing the Penguin
didn't understand. He didn't get humor
too well, either--

OFFICERS DONOHUE and O'MALLEY enter the bar, stereo-typically Irish-
looking. The place goes quiet, like a tomb.

                    MICKEY

Officer O'Mally. Officer Donohue. What
brings you here? Hope the radio ain't too
loud.

                    O'MALLEY
                (thick brogue)
          We're looking for someone, Mickey.

Donohue pulls a paper from his coat and shows it to the nearest BAR-FLY.

                    DONOHUE
                (thick brogue)
          You seen this fella?

INSERT - PAPER

An artist's rendition of the Penguin.

                                          BACK TO:

The patron shrugs.

The Penguin grabs Cooper's fedora and glasses and throws them on. He
grabs Cooper's cane and holds it up.

                    COOPER
          What did you do now?

The Penguin smiles like Stevie Wonder, swaying his head.

Mickey sneaks a peek at Donohue's bulletin.

                    MICKEY
          Looks like a penguin.

Donohue SNAPS the paper away.

                    O'MALLEY
          We know it's a penguin! This one's been
          causing problems all over the city.

                    MICKEY
          I saw that in the paper. Didn't he blow up
          a department store?

Cooper turns to the Penguin.

                    COOPER
          Did you blow up that department store?

The Penguin scratches his head, thinking.

                         MICKEY
                      (to O'Malley)
                  Have you checked the zoo?

                        O'MALLEY
                The zoo don't know anything about him.
                He's not one of theirs.

                         MICKEY
                Maybe them fool zoo people are behind
                this penguin. Maybe they let him out
                every night.

                        O'MALLEY
                  Why would they do that?

                         MICKEY
                Maybe they're training him for a robbery.
                I seen this movie once--

                        O'MALLEY
                  What?

                         MICKEY
                Is there any diamond exhibits coming to
                the Clover Museum soon?

O'Malley walks away, rolling his eyes.

                        O'MALLEY
                  Saints preserve me...

Donohue keeps out another drawing and shows it to another patron... the
Penguin in 'disguise.'

                        DONOHUE
                  Have you seen this penguin?

The Penguin tilts his head, as if trying to find a noise.

                        DONOHUE
                I'm sorry. I didn't realize... Hey Ian.
                C'mere!

O'Malley strolls up. Donohue holds up the drawing in the Penguin's face.

                        DONOHUE
                  Notice a resemblance?

O'Malley looks at the drawing. Then at the bird.

                    O'MALLEY
          Maybe. But this Penguin, here, is blind.

Donohue pulls O'Malley aside.

                    DONOHUE
                    (whispers)
          How do we know he's really blind?

                    O'MALLEY
          He's wearing dark glasses.

Donohue taps the Penguin on the shoulder. The Penguin looks around,
startled.

                    DONOHUE
          Excuse me, sir. Would you mind taking
          off your glasses?

The Penguin reaches for the glasses. Hesitates.

O'Malley puts his hand on his gun.

The Penguin removes the shades. His eyes have no pupils. They're yellow
and blank.

Donohue elbows O'Malley.

                    DONOHUE
                    (whispers)
          I told you he was blind.

O'Malley shows the drawing to Cooper.

                    O'MALLEY
          You there. Does this Penguin next to you
          look like this one here?

                    COOPER
          I don't see any resemblance.

                    DONOHUE
                    (to O'Malley)
          What did I tell you?

The Penguin turns away. His eyes roll down. A pained look floods his face.

Donohue tugs on O'Malley's arm.

                    DONOHUE

Let's get out of here. Our shift's almost
done.

Donohue taps the Penguin on the shoulder. The Penguin quickly puts the
glasses back on.

                    DONOHUE
          We apologize for bothering you.

The Penguin nods at the cops as they walk toward the door.

                    DONOHUE
          I could go for a drink. Get rid of this chill.

                    O'MALLEY
          Maybe we can come back here when
          we're done?

                    DONOHUE
              (laughing)
          Like I'd drink with these shines.

The two LAUGH as the door closes behind them.

The bar falls quiet. COUGHING is heard in the background. Cooper turns to
the Penguin.

                    COOPER
          Can I have my glasses back, now?

The Penguin smiles and sways his head, again.

                    COOPER (V.O.)
          I been hearing a lot about the Penguin
          since he arrived in town.

The two talk (MOS).

                    COOPER (V.O.)
          He been causing a lot of problems. For a
          lot of people.

The Penguin flaps his wings wildly. Cooper laughs. The Penguin sips his
drink and smiles.

                    COOPER (V.O.)
          But, for some reason, he was just the
          opposite with me.

Cooper pours the last of his beer in his mouth. His cheeks bulge. He taps the
Penguin on the shoulder.

Cooper raises his glass to his ear and pretends to pour.

The Penguin watches, fascinated. Cooper holds the glass below his mouth and squirts the beer inside.

The Penguin bursts out LAUGHING. He falls off his stool and hits the floor with a THUD.

The Penguin lays on the floor, GIGGLING.

                    COOPER (V.O.)
          I was his friend.

The Penguin looks up at Cooper. There's innocence and happiness on his face.

And he bursts out LAUGHING again.

EXT. DEERBORN STREET - DAY

Despite the fresh snow, the street still looks like shit.

                    COOPER (V.O.)
          And friends look out for each other.

INT. COOPER'S BEDROOM - CONTINUOUS

Cooper lays under blankets, his face buried in his pillow.

The room is sparsely furnished. A crucifix hangs over the bed. The saxophone case leans against the wall.

A toilet FLUSHES.

Cooper's lifeless eyes open. He lifts his head.

                    COOPER
          If that's who I think it is, you better light a
          match.

The Penguin steps from the bathroom, newspaper under his wing. He lights a match and tosses it back inside.

A fireball ROARS, just missing him.

He waddles into the bedroom. Cooper props himself up.

                    COOPER
          What time is it?

He reaches for a clock on the night stand and feels the hands.

> COOPER
> Eight-fifteen? Bird, don't you get hung
> over like regular people?

As Cooper puts the clock back, something falls off the night stand. He and the Penguin reach for it.

It's a dirty spoon.

> COOPER
> (nervous)
> I got it.

Cooper quickly tucks the spoon in a drawer.

> COOPER
> Just something I never put away.

Cooper shivers and gathers blankets under his chin. The Penguin watches him curiously.

> COOPER
> The landlord ain't putting the heat up,
> again. I guess you don't mind that,
> though.

The Penguin hops up on the window sill and WHINES at Cooper.

> COOPER
> Hold on, Bird. I can't hang with you right
> now. There's some personal business I
> gotta do.

The Penguin's face falls.

> COOPER
> I'll be by the park this morning. Why
> don't we meet then?

The Penguin drags himself past Cooper's bed, toward the exit.

> COOPER
> Now don't be all mopey like that.

The door SLAMS in the distance. Cooper drags himself out of bed.

> COOPER
> Don't be like this, Bird!

(muttering)
Damn bird. Like a spoiled child.

He leans against the door and SIGHS.

EXT. DEERBORN STREET - DAY

The Penguin drags his feet along the sidewalk. He crosses a street without looking--

BEEEEEEEEEEEEEEEEEP!

A truck SCREECHES to a halt, inches from the bird. The driver WAILS on his horn.

                    DRIVER
          Move it slowpoke!

The Penguin continues despondantly on his way.

                    CHINNY (O.S.)
          That's him.

                    WEE BILLY (O.S.)
          You sure it's that one, Chinny? Maybe it's
          another penguin.

Chinny and Wee Billy spy on the Penguin from an alleyway. Chinny's face is still bandaged.

                    CHINNY
          How many Penguins do you think are
          walking around here?

                    WEE BILLY
          I don't know. All penguins look alike to
          me.

A police car cruises by.

                    WEE BILLY (O.S.)
          See! Now, if that was the Penguin that
          messed up my suit, why didn't them cops
          arrest him?

                    CHINNY (O.S.)
          'Cause cops never do nothing in this
          neighborhood.

                    WEE BILLY (O.S.)

                    Damn straight. If that bird was in them
                    white neighborhoods, the cops would be
                    all over his feathery ass.

Chinny looks at Wee Billy. Realization floods his face.

                            WEE BILLY
                    I blame it all on the Jews.

                            CHINNY
                    You're right, Wee Billy.

                            WEE BILLY
                    I know. My gran'mama use to say Jews
                    are the reason black folk--

Chinny smacks him in the chest.

                            CHINNY
                    Not your dead gran'mama. White
                    neighborhoods! If that penguin screwed
                    around in white neighbor-hoods, every
                    cop in the city would be hunting him. You
                    brilliant!

They watch the Penguin walk away.

                            WEE BILLY
                        (nods to himself)
                    I'm brilliant. Yes, I am.

EXT. CLOVER PARK ENTRANCE - DAY

The entrance is gayly decorated. CREWS work on the tree. Cooper plays
Christmas music in his usual spot.

The Penguin walks up, a pouty expression on his face.

The bird listens. PASSERBYS stop and watch the performance.

People TAP their feet and smile. The music grows into a one-man symphony.
Cooper finishes to loud APPLAUSE.

People throw change into his case. Cooper tilts his hat and smiles from ear-
to-ear.

                            COOPER
                    Thank you very much. Merry Christmas!

The Penguin CLAPS too. He pulls bills from his pocket and tosses them in the case.

The others walk off, leave the Penguin and Cooper alone.

                    COOPER
          That you, Penguin? Thought I heard you.
          Your flippers clapping is a one-of-a-kind
          noise.

The Penguin looks at his flippers. He CLAPS a few times, listening intently to the sound.

                    COOPER
          C'mon over here.

The blind man ruffles the feathers on his head.

                    COOPER
          Sorry about this morning. I wasn't feeling
          right and I had some business that needed
          tending to.

The Penguin smiles a little.

                    COOPER
          How's the tree coming? They finish
          decorating it yet?

The Penguin GRUNTS.

                    COOPER
          You know, you might actually like
          Christmas if you gave it a chance.

The Penguin glances toward the tree again.

A life size Nativity scene sits nearby. Boxes are piled around, labeled 'MARY,' 'JOSEPH,' 'WISEMAN #1,' 'ANGEL,' etc.

The Penguin turns to Cooper and SIGHS.

                    COOPER
          I know you can be happy. You were
          feelin' the spirit last night at the bar.

The Penguin smiles a little.

                    COOPER

You found the fun in a joke. Find the fun
in Christmas--

Police cars race up the street, sirens BLARING.

                    COOPER
          What's the noise about? We got a fire
          somewhere?

The Penguin looks around and shrugs his shoulders.

                    COOPER
          Listen. I gotta be out here a little longer.
          How about getting us coffee?

Cooper plucks coins from his sax case, and holds them out.

                    COOPER
          Come on, Bird. I buy. You fly.

The Penguin quickly flaps his wings. He stands on his toes and strains to take
off.

                    COOPER
          Whaddaya say?

A CROWD gathers.

                    PEDESTRIAN 1 (V.O.)
          What's going on?

                    PEDESTRIAN 2 (V.O.)
          Didn't you hear?

                    PEDESTRIAN 3 (V.O.)
          Someone broke into the church. They
          stole the poor box!

The Penguin can't see through the crowd. He climbs up on the park's stone
wall.

Police cars surround a nearby church, surrounded by an incensed MOB.
Chinny and Wee Billy nearby, smiling impishly.

                    COOPER
          Who would steal from a church?

                    PEDESTRIAN 2 (V.O.)
          I'm gonna be sick!

                    PEDESTRIAN 1 (V.O.)

This close to Christmas!

Wee Billy scans the crowd. His eyes bug as he sees the bird. He taps Chinny on the shoulder.

                    CHINNY
          Not now, man.

                    WEE BILLY
          Now, man. Now!

Chinny follows Wee Billy's finger as he points.

                    CHINNY
          You gots to be kidding me...
               (shouting)
          That Penguin robbed the poor box! I seen
          him do it! And there he is!

He points to the bird.

                    COOPER
          The Penguin?

The Penguin looks at Chinny, surprised.

The crowd rushes forward. One MAN grabs the Penguin around the waist. The bird slips free and shoots up in the air.

The mob pushes Cooper into the wall.

                    COOPER
          Oof!

He hugs his sax tightly, protecting it.

People trample the sax case. Change falls down the grating.

The Penguin freaks. He reaches behind his back and--

PULLS OUT A TOMMYGUN!

He pumps the rifle with a loud CHI-CHUNK. The crowd GASPS.

                    COOPER
          No! Don't hurt them!

The Penguin looks at Cooper, lowers the rifle, when--

BLAM! BLAM! BLAM! BLAM!

Bullets WHIZ around the Penguin. One hits him in the shoulder.

Two COPS, O'SHEA and CLANCY (40s) muscle through the crowd, smoking revolvers in their hands.

The Penguin cradles his injury. The cops fire again.

BLAM! BLAM! BLAM!

The crowd scatters, terrified.

                    COOPER
          Nooo!

The Penguin leaps over the wall as bullets WHIZ by. Police whistles sound a SHRILL alarm.

O'Shea jumps the wall and looks around.

Clancy blows his whistle, then slips. The WHISTLING stops. He swallows hard and GAGS.

                    O'SHEA
               (brogue)
          Up, you shanty-laced bastard!

Clancy COUGHS and the whistle POPS out of his mouth. O'Shea stares down at him in disgust.

                    CLANCY
               (brogue)
          Do you see him?

                    O'SHEA
          No. But he left a trail.

O'Shea points to flipper-shaped tracks in the snow. Every few feet, drops of blood.

EXT. CLOVER PARK ENTRANCE - CONTINUOUS

The Penguin runs frantically through the snow. Police whistles SCREAM in the distance.

He trips over a rock and falls down an ice-covered hill. He belly slides, picks up speed.

Kids on sleds 'OOH' and 'AAH.'

He hits the bottom and slides to a stop by a frozen lake.

The wounded bird staggers to his feet. Presses snow to his shoulder and HISSES in pain.

A giggling EIGHT YEAR OLD BOY on a snow disk slides up to him. They look at each other in a moment of silence.

EXT. CLOVER PARK ENTRANCE - CONTINUOUS

SPECTATORS crowd along the wall where the Penguin disappeared. Cooper stands among the crowd.

                    WEE BILLY (O.S.)
          Man, this is workin' better than we
          thought.

Cooper cocks his head, listening. Chinny and Wee Billy whisper to each other a few feet away, grinning.

                    CHINNY
          All of Clover City's gonna be after that
          bird 'cause of what we done.

                    WEE BILLY
          City's gonna give him a whipping. Just
          like the time my gran'mama caught me
          going into her purse--

                    CHINNY
          We don't need to hear about your dead
          gran'mama.

Wee Billy's smile disappears.

                    CHINNY
          Let's get back to Candletown. We got
          business to conduct.

They walk off. Cooper 'watches' them, a frown on his face.

EXT. CLOVER PARK LAKE - CONTINUOUS

The Penguin races across the frozen lake, COPS on his 'tail.' He slides past startled skaters with grace.

He whips a pistol out and aims behind him at the bumbling COPS slipping and falling on their asses.

                    O'SHEA

                    (shouting)
          Come on! Up, you drunken shanty-laced
          bastards!

The Penguin lowers his gun and slides away, smiling.

Twenty feet from the shore, his smile disappears.

A dozen COPS wait on the edge, pistols drawn.

SGT. QUINN stands in front, revolver in hand.

                    QUINN
          Freeze, Penguin!

The Penguin raises an eyebrow. Another COP snickers. Quinn glares at him,
pissed.

                    COP
          You said *freeze* to a penguin... On ice--

                    QUINN
          Shut up!
                    (to Penguin)
          We have you surrounded! Put your gun
          down!

The Penguin slides to a stop. The cops following behind catch up.

                    QUINN
          Surrender, Penguin! I'm giving you to the
          count of three!

The Penguin looks around. There's no escape.

                    QUINN
          One!

PEOPLE gather. PARENTS cling tightly to their KIDS.

                    QUINN
          Two!

The Penguin slowly lowers his gun. The cops on the shore slowly close in.

                    QUINN
          That's right, Penguin. Down.

The cop next to Quinn breathes a SIGH of relief until--

BLAMM!!

The Penguin shoots around his feet, creates a hole in the ice that swallows him up.

His dark silhouette swims like a torpedo under the ice.

The cops wildly shoot wildly at him.

BLAMBLAMBLAMBLAMBLAMBLAMBLAM--!

Bullets punch holes in the ice. It CRACKS and breaks under the surprised cops' feet. They plunge into the water.

The Penguin swims away. His movements, underwater ballet.

EXT. LAKESIDE - MINUTES LATER

The police pull themselves out. O'Shea hauls the shivering Clancy out of the water.

                    O'SHEA
          Up, you drunken shanty-laced bastard--!

Clancy yanks him into the water with a loud SPLASH.

                    CLANCY
               (mocking)
          Up, you drunken shanty-laced bastard!
          Up, you drunken shanty-laced bastard!
               (normal)
          Been listening to you say that for nine
          whole years. I'm tired of it!

In the distance, a BAND plays in a pavilion. SKATERS glide to the music, ignoring the comical scene as they skate to the music. Norman Rockwell would proud--

BOOM!!

Ice in front of the pavilion EXPLODES. Everyone runs for cover. Chunks rain from the sky.

The Penguin steps onto the shore. He drags behind him a bazooka and a trail of blood.

He leans against a tree and examines his wounds. Lets out a pain-filled SIGH.

EXT. THE GREAT HALL RESTAURANT - LATER

PEOPLE hustle and bustle along the sidewalk.

CHINNY (V.O.)
Now this is what I'm talkin' about!

WEE BILLY (V.O.)
Yeah, this is what we're talkin' about,
alright!

INT. THE GREAT HALL RESTAURANT - CONTINUOUS

Chinny and Wee Billy look around, amazed. The restaurant is empty. An
ELDERLY MAN slowly sweeps the floor.

CHINNY
Even the dirt in this place is high class.
With that penguin gone, this is where
we're gonna be.

WEE BILLY
No more eating food from automats.

CHINNY
No more Mickey's grilled cheese
sandwiches!

Chinny leans against the bar, looking proud.

CHINNY
It'll be prime rib and champagne from
now on.

TERRENCE (O.S.)
(thick brogue)
We're not looking for kitchen help.

Chinny and Wee Billy spin around.

Terrence the bartender steps from a door, carrying two cases of scotch. A
cigarette hangs from his mouth.

He puts the scotch on the bar.

WEE BILLY
Kitchen help?

TERRENCE
You the boys working for Mister Hall in
Candletown? Had your asses handed to
you by a wee bird?

                         WEE BILLY
               He wasn't that little--

                         TERRENCE
               Did he use his flippers to cut you up like
               that? Or did he peck you with his little
               beak?

                         CHINNY
                    (bossy)
               Tell Mister Hall that Chinny Monroe and
               Wee Billy Jefferson are here to see him,
               boy.

Terrence grabs Chinny's tie and yanks. Chinny's chin hits the bar. The
Irishman pulls a dagger from his boot. He stabs it through Chinny's tie,
pinning him down.

                         TERRENCE
               Call me 'boy' again and I'll carry you home
               so your family can watch me skin you.
               Understand me, shine?

                         HALL (O.C.)
               Terrence, that's no way to treat business
               associates.

Hall walks down the stairs, conservatively dressed. He lights a cigar. Savors
it.

                         HALL
               Misters Monroe and Jefferson are here at
               my request.

Terrence pulls his knife from the bar. Chinny jumps away. Wee Billy hides
behind him, shivering.

                         HALL
               Gentlemen, I do not have much time. To
               my office, please.

INT. GREGORY HALL'S OFFICE - MOMENTS LATER

Hall relaxes behind his desk. Chinny and Wee Billy sit opposite him.

                         CHINNY
               We appreciate you seeing us on short
               notice, Mister Hall--

WEE BILLY

Yes we do--

CHINNY

But we don't appreciate being
disrespected by your staff--

WEE BILLY

No we don't--

HALL

Shut up.

Chinny and Wee Billy stare at him, stunned.

HALL

When we first discussed business, you
were told to enter my restaurant through
the kitchen.

CHINNY

Well, yes--

HALL

Don't you think people would get
suspicious if they saw coloreds coming
into The Great Hall through the front?

CHINNY
(through gritted teeth)
You're right. But that don't give your
bartender no right--

HALL

Terrence was very gentle with you
downstairs. Consider it a warning.

CHINNY

We ain't afraid of no bartender, Mister
Hall.

HALL

You should be. Terrence is an Irish
nationalist. Wanted for questioning in the
bombings of several British installations...
And the murder of forty soldiers.

WEE BILLY

Forty?

                    HALL
          Watching your parents die at the hands of
          British soldiers does a lot to a boy. None
          of it good.

Chinny and Wee Billy look at each other, nervously.

                    HALL
          Now then. You mentioned *good* news on
          the telephone...

EXT. DEERBORN STREET - NIGHT

The last of the sun's rays slip away.

                    COOPER (V.O.)
          The mayor all but closed the park down,
          after what happened.

INT. COOPER'S BEDROOM - CONTINUOUS

Cooper sits by a window, playing his sax in the dark.

                    COOPER (V.O.)
          I didn't feel like working after that, so I
          came home. Half-expected him to be
          here. But he wasn't.

The music lights up the dreary night with warmth and soul.

                    COOPER (V.O.)
          So I invited him.

A candle appears in windows across the street. Several more light up. One
by one.

                    COOPER (V.O.)
          Most people think Candletown got its
          name 'cause people here can't pay their
          electric bills.

People place candles in windows.

                    COOPER (V.O.)
          But it ain't so. Newspapers dreamed up
          the name during the first World War...

Candles brighten doorways, animate the street with flickering shadows.

                    COOPERS (V.O.)
          Clover City sent a lot of boys over to
          Europe. People lit so many candles the
          church ran out of them. So people
          brought their own.

More candles. Everywhere.

                    COOPER (V.O.)
          When the church ran out of room, they
          were lit in the street. Eventually, the
          whole city ran out of candles just 'cause
          one small neighborhood prayed so much-
          -

The floor CREAKS behind Cooper. He turns his head.

                    COOPER
               Is that you...?

The Penguin leans against the doorway. Looks like shit. He clutches his
wound and mouths some words.

                    COOPER (V.O.)
               'Help me...' he said.

The Penguin falls to the floor.

                    COOPER (V.O.)
               I wasn't sure if he was asking me for help,
               or ordering me to.

Cooper puts his sax down and hurries over.

                    COOPER (V.O.)
               It didn't matter...

He picks up the Penguin and carries him to the bed. Cooper smells his
fingers.

                    COOPER
               Blood?

The Penguins GRUNTS.

Cooper's hand gently glides across the Penguin's flipper.

It bends around his fingers and holds on tight.

                    COOPER (V.O.)

Didn't know if he was gonna live or die. I
wasn't no animal doctor.

The Penguin looks at Cooper with half closed eyes.

                    COOPER
          How bad is it?

                    COOPER (V.O.)
          "They winged me," he told me.

Cooper's lips curl in a faint smile. The Penguin weakly smiles back.

He starts to say something, but stops and SIGHS. He bows his head in quiet
shame.

                    COOPER (V.O.)
          "You want to ask me something," he said.
          "About the church?"

Cooper stares at the bird.

                    COOPER
          If you say you didn't do it, I'll believe you.

                    COOPER (V.O.)
          "I didn't," he said.

Cooper smiles.

                    COOPER (V.O.)
          The bird gave me his word. And that was
          good enough for me.

EXT. DEERBORN STREET - LATER

Chinny and Wee Billy walk slowly along the street. They tighten their coat
collars against the wind.

                    WEE BILLY
          Can't believe how cold it got.

                    CHINNY
          Forget the cold. If we don't get Mister
          Hall his money, things are gonna get hot
          for us.

                    WEE BILLY
          How we supposed to raise nine hundred
          dollars in two days?

They bump an elderly MAN out of their way. He totter and tumbles into the snow.

> CHINNY
> Yeah. Thanks to that penguin.

Wee Billy points ahead.

> WEE BILLY
> Hey, lookit there!

Candles shine along the street.

> CHINNY
> So what? Folks ain't paid their electric
> bills, is all.

Sax MUSIC floats through the air.

> CHINNY
> Saxophone music? I got me an idea.

INT. COOPER'S BEDROOM - MOMENTS LATER

Cooper plays in the dark bedroom. The Penguin rests in bed, deep in thought.

A KNOCK on the door.

The music continues.

Insistent KNOCKING once again.

Cooper stops playing.

> COOPER
> Who in the world?

He puts the sax down.

INT. COOPER'S APARTMENT - FRONT DOOR - CONTINUOUS

The apartment is dark. Cooper cracks open his apartment door. A sliver of light shines through.

> COOPER
> Who's there?

> CHINNY (O.S.)

It's us, Cooper...

Chinny and Wee Billy stand in the hallway.

                    COOPER
          Chinny?

                    CHINNY
          We need to talk, my man.

                    COOPER
          This ain't a good time--

Chinny shoves the door open and storms inside.

                    CHINNY
          Ain't a good time for none of us.

Chinny pins Cooper against the wall.

                    COOPER
          What do you think you're doing?

                    CHINNY
          Listen, old man. We need money and we
          know you got some.

                    COOPER
          I ain't got nothing.

                    CHINNY
          Don't mess with me! This is your busy
          season and you been buying stuff from us-
          -

Wee Billy feels the wall.

                    WEE BILLY
          Where the light switch?

                    COOPER
          Do I look like I need one?

Chinny SLAPS Cooper across the face.

                    CHINNY
          Where's the light switch, old man?

                    COOPER
          The switch is in the ceiling. Look for the
          string.

Wee Billy pulls the string. A weak bulb flickers on. The door CREAKS shut.

The apartment hallway is empty except for a table and chair.

                    CHINNY
          So where's the money?

                    COOPER
          It ain't here! Been putting' it into bonds
          and my bank account.

Wee Billy walks to the card table. A cigar box rests on top.

                    WEE BILLY
          The bank? Sounds risky to me.

He opens the box and pulls out a bank book.

                    WEE BILLY
          Clover City Federal Saving?

                    COOPER
          That's mine! Now put it down and get
          out!

Chinny grabs the book and flips through it.

                    CHINNY
          Forty-four hundred dollars!

                    COOPER
          Give me that!

Cooper flails around and pulls it from Chinny's hand.

                    COOPER
          After all I done for you boys, you should
          be ashamed! Chinny, you used to come
          here and hide from your daddy when he
          was drinking.

Chinny shoots him a dirty look.

                    COOPER
          And Wee Billy. You use to come to me
          whenever Miss Sophie was sick.

                    WEE BILLY
          You always was nice to my gran'mama.

                    CHINNY
          Enough with your dead gran'mama! And
          enough bullshit, old man! You always got
          money when you come see us. How come
          you don't got it now?

                    COOPER
          You can't have it!

He pushes Chinny. The gesture's weak; Chinny barely moves.

Chinny shoves back. Cooper hits the table and CRASHES to the floor.

Chinny holds a switchblade to the old man's cheek.

                    CHINNY
          If you don't give it to me, I'm gonna make
          your face look like mine!

                    COOPER
          What?

                    CHINNY
          You heard me!

                    COOPER
          I heard you. You just... that didn't make
          no sense.

                    WEE BILLY
          The man's blind, Chinny. He can't see
          what your face looks like--

                    CHINNY
          Shut up!

                    WEE BILLY
          Maybe you should try a different threat--

                    CHINNY
          We're taking your money, old man. And
          nobody's gonna stop us, you hear...?

The floor CREAKS.

The Penguin stands there, a bloodied bandage on one flipper. There's a
DOUBLE-BARREL SHOTGUN in the other!

                    WEE BILLY
          Oh shit.

The bird cocks the hammers back on the rifle, smiling. Wee Billy stares at him, bug-eyed.

CLICK-CLICK

                         WEE BILLY
              Chinny? What should we do, man...?

Racing FOOTSTEPS are heard. Wee Billy turns as the apartment door CREAKS shut.

Chinny's gone! Without a trace!

EXT. APARTMENT STAIRWELL - MOMENTS LATER

A ROAR echoes through the stairwell.

Wee Billy races down the stairs. The wall over his head EXPLODES.

The Penguin stands at the landing and reloads.

Cooper hurries down the stairs (as fast as he can).

                         COOPER
              Penguin! Where are you, bird?

The Penguin WHISTLES. Cooper stops next to him.

                         COOPER
              Are you crazy? What the hell you doing
              shooting up the place like this?

The Penguin mouths the words:

                         COOPER (V.O.)
              "Protecting a friend," he told me.

They look at each other in a moment of understanding.

EXT. DEERBORN STREET - CONTINUOUS

Wee Billy races comically from the building.

He slams into a MAN, carrying a bag. The contents fly in the air. The Man hits the ground.

                         MAN
              Oof!

Wee Billy swings down an alley. He pratfalls and slides on his back. He SLAMS into a wall, legs up in the air.

He grabs his chest, PANTING. Sheer terror paints his face.

                    CHINNY (O.S.)
          You get him?

Chinny lays a few feet away, in an identical pose.

INT. COOPER'S HALLWAY - CONTINUOUS

Cooper and the Penguin walk to his apartment. The adjacent apartment door opens a crack.

MISS CLARA (80) a scrawny woman with Coke bottle glasses, sticks her grey head outside.

                    MISS CLARA
          Cooper? That you?

She stares blankly ahead of her.

                    COOPER
          Yes, Miss Clara.

EDVENA (5) appears at Clara's side. She holds a squirming kitten and a candy cane.

                    MISS CLARA
          Was that gunfire I just heard?

                    COOPER
          No, Miss Clara. A light bulb fell on the
          floor.

He opens his apartment door.

                    MISS CLARA
          Oh my. Somebody should clean that up.
          Before somebody gets hurt.

The girl sticks the candy cane in her mouth and waves to the Penguin. He looks at her. She blows him a kiss.

Puzzled, the Penguin backs away and escapes through Cooper's open door.

EXT. DEERBORN STREET - NIGHT

Chinny stands in a telephone both. Wee Billy paces nearby.

                    CHINNY
              (into phone)
         I know I told you that the police killed the
         penguin, Mister Hall--

                    WEE BILLY
         Lemme talk to him.

Wee Billy steps up. Chinny waves him away.

                    CHINNY
         But he ain't dead. We just seen him here
         in Candletown--

                    WEE BILLY
         Penguin's gonna be the death of us.

                    CHINNY
         Yes, Mister Hall. I know, sir--

                    WEE BILLY
         Lemme talk to him. Lemme talk--

Chinny pushes him back.

                    CHINNY
         But there's more, Mister Hall...

                    WEE BILLY
         That ain't no penguin if you ask me. He's
         really a midget in a tuxedo with machine
         guns--

                    CHINNY
         The penguin found out we was getting
         our drugs from you, sir.

                    WEE BILLY
              (shocked)
         What?

                    CHINNY
         I don't know how he found out, Mister
         Hall. Me and Wee Billy didn't tell him
         squat.

Wee Billy jumps around the booth, trying to get Chinny's attention.

                         WEE BILLY
            You crazy? You gonna go lying like that?

                          CHINNY
            His exact words to me and Wee Billy was,
            'Tell Gregory Hall I'm coming for him!'

Wee Billy keeps jumping. His muffled SCREAMS barely heard.

                          CHINNY
            I know I have a good deal with you, sir,
            but we have good news, too.

Wee Billy TAPS repeatedly on the glass and SCREAMS (MOS).

                          CHINNY
            We know where he's hiding out.

INT. COOPER'S BEDROOM - CONTINUOUS

Cooper helps the Penguin into bed.

                          COOPER
            You like making enemies, don't you?

The Penguin GRUNTS.

                          COOPER
            Anything I can get you?

                       COOPER (V.O.)
            "Screaming Turkey," he told me... I
            thought the poor bird was gonna drink
            himself to death.

Cooper walks to a nearby closet and opens it. Tattered coats hang inside.
Liquor bottles cover the floor.

                       COOPER (O.S.)
            Then he asked for a needle and thread.

Cooper turns to him, confused.

INT. COOPER'S BEDROOM - LATER

Cooper holds a table lamp over the Penguin. The Penguin gulps whiskey and
pours some on his wounds, grimacing.

He pulls a stiletto from his 'back pocket.' He picks at his wound and GRUNTS through clenched teeth.

                    COOPER (V.O.)
          He was fixing himself up. It's a good thing
          I couldn't watch.

The Penguin pulls the dagger out and tosses it aside.

He sticks his beak into his flipper. He twists and turns, fishing around.

The bird lifts his bloodied head and spits.

The spent bullet bounces on the floor--

TING!

He drinks from the bottle yet again.

EXT. COOPER'S APARTMENT BUILDING - LATER

Snow glistens in the street. SOFT JAZZ is heard.

                    COOPER (V.O.)
          The Penguin stitched himself up after
          that. He must've done it right 'cause he
          survived.

INT. COOPER'S BEDROOM - CONTINUOUS

Cooper plays saxophone on the bed. The Penguin rests.

                    COOPER (V.O.)
          I guess his skills included fixing things as
          well as destroying them. Quite an
          amazing little bird.

The Penguin looks at him.

                    COOPER (V.O.)
          "Cooper?" he called.

Cooper stops playing.

                    COOPER (V.O.)
          "Do you want to know why I hate
          Christmas..? 'Cuz it killed my family."

Cooper shoots him a respectful look.

EXT. BREISS CITY ZOO - DAY

Cages as far as the eye can see. The ground is spotless. American flags fly
overhead.

                    COOPER (V.O.)
          The bird told me about a zoo in Kent,
          Virginia. Where he was born.

MOTHERS lead their CHILDREN to a large grey building. The sign overhead
reads:

THE PENGUIN HOUSE

The exhibit is elaborate, resembling a South Pole landscape. PEOPLE watch
PENGUINS waddle about. Squat little birds with YELLOW EYES.

                    COOPER (V.O.)
          He didn't remember that much...

Two ADULT MACARONI PENGUINS stand at the water's edge. A YOUNG
PENGUIN slides up to them and nuzzles between the two.

                    COOPER (V.O.)
          But he remembered being loved.

EXT. BREISS CITY ZOO - DAY

The grounds are almost empty. The few humans left wear green zoo
uniforms.

                    COOPER (V.O.)
          Problem was, the war was hurting zoo
          business. They weren't getting visitors
          like they use to.

INT. CONFERENCE ROOM - CONTINUOUS

A DISTINGUISHED-LOOKING MAN stares out a window, glum.

A DOZEN BUSINESSMEN sit around a conference table. Charts rest on easels.
Graph lines and charts spiral downward.

                    COOPER (V.O.)
          Things only got worse from there...

EXT. BREISS CITY ZOO ENTRANCE - DAY

A hand-painted sign hangs over the entrance:

CLOSED UNTIL FURTHER NOTICE

Children turn away, sad looks on their little faces.

                    COOPER (V.O.)
              The zoo ended up closing.

Flatbed trucks pull away from the zoo.

DANGER: LIVE ANIMALS is posted on the sides of the trucks. Tons of cages
are stacked in the back.

                    COOPER (V.O.)
              The penguins were all supposed to go to
              some zoo in New York--

The Young Penguin stares from his cage, horrified.

                    COOPER (V.O.)
              But, one got separated.

Another truck is stuffed with caged PENGUINS. The Young Penguin's parents
press against the bars.

The trucks separate at an intersection.

                    COOPER (V.O.)
              He never saw his family again.

EXT. CLOVER CITY ZOO - DAY

The truck rolls through a dirty service entrance. Rain POUNDS down on
every side.

                    COOPER (V.O.)
              Six days later, the truck arrived in Clover
              City, not stopping once during it's cross-
              country trip.

The truck backs up to a loading dock. Zoo employees, wearing red matching
coats and pants, climb onto the truck.

                    COOPER (V.O.)
              The animals weren't fed or watered.
              Many died. Or close to it.

One WORKER pulls a tarp off a cage, jumps back in horror. A SNARLING wolf stands over its half-eaten mate.

Cages are yanked from the truck. A dead seal is thrown in a filthy dumpster.

A FEMALE ZOOKEEPER opens a tiny cage. The Young Penguin lays inside, shivering.

She shakes her head and walks away.

                    COOPER (V.O.)
          The worst part was, no one cared.

INT. CLOVER CITY ZOO PENGUIN HOUSE - LATER

The Young Penguin is sprayed with a pressure hose. He's knocked down by the blast.

                    COOPER (V.O.)
          As quickly as he arrived, the little Penguin
          was cleaned up--

INT. PENGUIN EXHIBIT - LATER

A cinder block room, crudely painted with Arctic murals. The water is covered in a layer of scum.

A metal door slides open and the Young Penguin is shoved through. He lands on his face. The door SLAMS shut.

                    COOPER (V.O.)
          And put on display.

The Young Penguin waddles over to TWO PENGUINS and smile. They stare at him and turn away.

The Young Penguin's smile fades.

                    COOPER (V.O.)
          In a place he wasn't wanted--

An ELDERLY PENGUIN, stands in a corner. The Young Penguin nuzzles against him.

The Elderly Penguin spins around, startled. His eyes are blank white. His head darts around.

The Young Penguin backs away, horrified.

                         COOPER (V.O.)
                    And didn't want to be.

The Elderly Penguin SNIFFS the air.

A CREAK is heard. All the penguins spin toward the door.

                         BLACK BOOTS (O.S.)
                      (slurred; muffled)
                    Here's your food, stupid birds.

A pair of BLACK BOOTS shuffle into the room. A bucket hangs next to them.

The penguins shy away. Small fish pelt their back.

                         BLACK BOOTS (O.S.)
                    And stop shitting in your pool. I'm tired
                    of cleaning it.

The Young Penguin starts waddling over. The Elderly Penguin pulls him
back.

The bucket of fish pours onto the floor. Black Boots kicks fish at the birds.

'Boots' walks outside and SLAMS the door.

The Elderly Penguin releases the Young Penguin who darts to the food. He
gulps some down. Then stops.

The youngster brings the elderly penguin a fish. The Elderly Penguin takes it
and eats.

                         COOPER (V.O.)
                    The Young Penguin did the best he could.

The Young Penguin retrieves more fish. He nuzzles under the older bird's
wing.

                         COOPER (V.O.)
                    And it wasn't long before he made a
                    friend.

INT. PENGUIN EXHIBIT - DAY

The two Penguins huddle in the corner.

                         COOPER (V.O.)
                    The young penguin's fears settled down
                    as he embraced his new family.

Other penguins waddle around, not paying attention to anyone.

INT. PENGUIN EXHIBIT - LATER

Penguins hang out. CREAKING is heard, followed by HEAVY FOOT STEPS.
Black Boots walks inside.

                    BLACK BOOTS (O.S.)
                  (slurred; muffled)
            Dinner time, you stupid birds.

A hand throws fish at the cringing penguins. Black Boots walks away.

The Young Penguin (now bigger) carries food to his friend.

The old bird smells it and frowns. He drops the fish, untouched on the floor.

                    COOPER (V.O.)
            But then it started all over again.

The Young Penguin offers fish again. The Old Penguin SIGHS and walks
away. The Young Penguin's face falls.

                    COOPER (V.O.)
              He was losing his family.

The Young Penguin's face falls. He looks confused.

EXT. CLOVER CITY ZOO - DAY

ZOO EMPLOYEES hang ratty-looking Christmas decorations. Everyone is
dressed in red uniforms.

INT. PENGUIN EXHIBIT - LATER

Penguins gather in the corner.

The Young Penguin pushes through them, horrified.

The Elderly Penguin lays on the ground. Doesn't move.

The Young Penguin lifts his head. It rolls limply in his flipper.

A tear streaks down his face. CREAKING is heard.

                    BLACK BOOTS (O.S.)
                  (slurred; muffled)

                    Alright, stupid birds. Here's your friggin'
                    breakfast--

Black Boots walks over. The other birds immediately scatter.

                         BLACK BOOTS (O.S.)
                    What's this? A sick bird?

Black Boots nudges the Elderly Penguin with a foot. No response.

Boots kicks the body. The Young Penguin looks on, shocked.

                         BLACK BOOTS (O.S.)
                    He ain't sick. He's dead. Stupid dead bird.

The Young Penguin shakes his head: a panicked 'no.'

Black Boots crouches down. His rotund ass shoves the Young Penguin aside.

                         BLACK BOOTS
                    Don't need no damn kids seeing no dead
                    penguin in here.

The Young Penguin inches toward his friend. A pudgy hand slaps him away,
knocking him down.

                         BLACK BOOTS
                    Outta the way, stupid bird!

The Young Penguin stares at the handler, a fat man with a dirty white beard.
He resembles a SLOPPY SANTA CLAUS.

Boots grabs the Elderly Penguin and sits him up.

                         BLACK BOOTS
                    Your dead friend's coming with me.
                         (to Elderly Penguin)
                    You gonna come home with me?

He puppeteers the Elderly Penguin's head.

                         BLACK BOOTS
                         (high-pitched)
                    Don't take me away! You'll eat me!
                         (regular voice)
                    That's right! Nothing beats a roasted
                    penguin dinner!
                         (high-pitched)
                    No! Not roasted penguin dinner!

Black Boots bursts out in a maniacal HO HO HO.

An arched uni-brow forms over the Young Penguin's eyes. His pupils turns bloody red. He lunges forward and CHOMPS on Black Boots' hand.

Black Boots HOWLS and backhands the youngster--

> BLACK BOOTS
> --Stupid bird--!

--CRACK--

The Young Penguin hits his head against the wall.

Black Boots pulls a switchblade knife from his pocket...

The Young Penguin lifts his head. There's blood on the wall and between his eyes.

> BLACK BOOTS
> I'll be taking two of your corpses out
> today!

The Young Penguin grabs fish from the ground and twirls them like nunchuks. Around the body. Under flippers. Over his sleek penguin head.

Black Boots closes in. The Young Penguin throws the fish, and clocks him in the eyes.

Black Boots staggers back.

> BLACK BOOTS
> I'll make a friggin' hat outta you!

Black Boots steps on a fish. He slips and pancakes on the floor. The knife flies out of his hand.

The two look at the knife. And each other.

The Young Penguin leaps. Grabs the knife in a mid-air somersault, and sticks it in the zookeeper's hand.

Black Boots HOWLS.

The Young Penguin lands by the water's edge. Black Boots pulls the knife from his hand and rushes the bird.

The Penguin grabs Black Boot's arm. The man flips into the water. He thrashes around.

> BLACK BOOTS
> Help! Help! I can't swim!

He sinks beneath the scum-covered surface and disappears.

The Young Penguin hurries to the Elderly Penguin's side and holds him tenderly. Tears roll down his cheeks.

He turns to the other birds for help.

> COOPER (V.O.)
> And that's when he realized--

The penguins mill around, oblivious.

> COOPER (V.O.)
> That he was truly alone in this world.

He kisses his friend's forehead and puts him down.

The Young Penguin crosses the exhibit and picks up the knife. The metal door CREAKS open. Then SLAMS shut.

The other penguins continue to eat. An ice-covered hand bobs at the water's edge.

INT. COOPER'S BEDROOM - NIGHT

Cooper sits next to his friend, holding the bottle of Screaming Turkey. The room's as quiet as a tomb.

> COOPER (V.O.)
> Then he told me about his weapons.
> Knives. Guns. Poisons of every kind.
> Explosives.

He brings the bottle to his lips and swallows hard.

> COOPER (V.O.)
> He could kill every man, woman and child
> in Clover City if he wanted to. God help
> me if I ever repeat where this bird got it
> all. Or where he keeps it.

INT. GREGORY HALL'S OFFICE - DAY

Hall hangs up the phone. He leans back in his chair and plays with his cigar.

> HALL
> Commissioner McDonald is dispatching
> his best men to Mister Cooper's home.

Terrence sits in a chair across from Hall.

                    HALL
          I want you there. This penguin cannot
          survive the night.

                    TERRENCE
          What about the coloreds?

                    HALL
          More trouble than they're worth. Take
          care of the bird. Then take care of them.

                    TERRENCE
          Yes, sir.

Terrence quietly leaves. Hall draws deeply on his cigar.

INT. COOPER'S KITCHEN - NIGHT

A stove burner provides the only light. Cooper fills two coffee cups.

INT. COOPER'S BEDROOM - CONTINUOUS

Cooper puts a cup down on the night table. The Penguin sits up in the bed.

                    COOPER
          I don't use cream or sugar, myself.

The Penguin bobs his beak in his cup.

                    COOPER (V.O.)
          Then the awkward silence began. I didn't
          have anything to say. But I knew he did.

The Penguin looks at Cooper.

                    COOPER (V.O.)
          He asked me about Chinny and Wee Billy.

Cooper hangs his head low.

                    COOPER (V.O.)
          He asked about the syringe and the spoon.
          I couldn't lie, not to him.

Cooper walks toward the window and puts his mug on the sill. He faces the
Penguin.

COOPER (V.O.)
Been using the stuff twenty years. Used
to buy it from a guy named Rico. Now it
was Chinny and Wee Billy.

Cooper waves his hands around, pleads his case.

COOPER (V.O.)
I told him I wasn't like the others. Used it
only when my arthritis was bothering me
fierce.

The Penguin stares at him.

COOPER (V.O.)
Couldn't play with my fingers tight. And
when I can't play, I can't pay my rent.
Can't even eat.

The Penguin's expression doesn't change.

COOPER
Say something!

RED FLASHING LIGHTS flicker outside the window.

COOPER (V.O.)
"We have company," he said.

EXT. COOPER'S BUILDING - CONTINUOUS

Police cars and vans pull up. Uniformed OFFICERS climb out.

INT. COOPER'S BEDROOM - CONTINUOUS

The Penguin and Cooper look at each other.

COOPER
What do we do?

The Penguin shuts off the lamp. The room is dark, lit only by red flashes.

COOPER (V.O.)
"Go next door," he said. "Where it's safe."

EXT. COOPER'S WINDOW - THROUGH CROSSHAIRS

The Penguin turns the light off. Red flashing lights illuminate the night.

EXT. ROOF TOP - CONTINUOUS

A figure lies on the rooftop edge, rifle in hand. He lowers the rifle from his face. It's Terrence.

                    TERRENCE
          Goddamn birdie.

He watches the cops rush inside.

DING DONG!

INT. COOPER'S APARTMENT BUILDING - CONTINUOUS

Cooper presses his neighbor's doorbell.

DING DONG!

The door opens. Miss Clara's eyes peer over the chain.

                    MISS CLARA
          Heaven's Cooper! What are you doing
          here at this hour?

                    COOPER
          I, er, heard the police outside and I
          wanted to be sure you were okay.

                    MISS CLARA
          The police? Dear me.

                    COOPER
          Wouldn't be neighborly if I didn't check
          on you.

                    MISS CLARA
          Thank you, Cooper. I was about to put
          some tea on. Would you care for a cup?

                    COOPER
          That would be lovely, Miss Clara.

She removes the chain and opens the door.

                    MISS CLARA
          Come in, please.

Cooper walks in. The door closes gently behind him.

UNIFORMED OFFICERS race up the stairs, a red-headed sergeant leads the way.

                    RED-HEADED SERGEANT
               (whispering)
          Shh! If this bird gets away, the
          Commissioner will have our shields.

They tip-toe to Cooper's door. The sergeant puts his ear to the door.

He waves to his men. Mouths the words:

ONE. TWO. THREE.

The cops BUST the door down and rush into darkness. CRASHING and BREAKING fill the room.

                    COP (V.O.)
          Where're the lights?

                    COP 3 (V.O.)
          Oww! What the hell--?

                    COP 4 (V.O.)
          Get off me!

                    O'SHEA (V.O.)
          Get up, you drunken shanty-laced
          bastards!

                    CLANCY (V.O.)
          Blow it out your arse, O'Shea!

                    COP 5 (V.O.)
          I see him!

                    COP 6 (V.O.)
          Shoot him! Shoot him!

                    RED-HEADED SERGEANT (V.O.)
          Nobody shoot!

GUNFIRE echoes through the building. It doesn't stop.

INT. MISS CLARA'S BEDROOM - CONTINUOUS

The room is sparsely furnished.

Little Edvena sits on the bed. She clings tightly to her cat. Muffled gunfire RATTLES next door.

Bullets rip through the wall.

The Penguin crashes through the sheetrock and lands on his feet. He fires a pistol through the hole--

BLAM BLAM BLAM

He looks at the girl, surprised. She blinks back, terrified.

He opens a closet door and throws the girl and cat in.

He shuts the door and flips the mattress against it. Bullets shred the underside.

INT. CLOSET - CONTINUOUS

Muffled GUNFIRE is heard outside. The girl hugs her pet even tighter to her chest.

                    EDVENA
          The funny bird saved us, Snyder...

She huddles safely in the small dark space.

INT. MISS CLARA'S KITCHEN - CONTINUOUS

Cooper and Miss Clara sit around the table. Muffled GUNFIRE is heard.

                    MISS CLARA
          Did you hear that Gina-Lee moved back
          home?

                    COOPER
          Matter of fact, I did. Poor girl.

Bullets RIP through the wall. Glassware SHATTERS. Plaster falls onto the table.

Miss Clara brings her cup to her lips. A bullet shatters it.

                    MISS CLARA
          This wouldn't be happening if they had
          coloreds on the force.

                    COOPER
          You may have a point, there.

EXT. ROOF TOP - CONTINUOUS

Terrence sits on his perch. Muzzle flashes light up Cooper's apartment like fireflies.

                    TERRENCE
          Bye-bye, little birdie.

The clouds break. The moon shines through. Something small patters across the roof.

                    TERRENCE
          Eh?

A silhouette stands on the roof's edge. It aims a strange rifle at the street and squeezes the trigger--

THWIPP!

A grappling hook flies through the air, tethered by cable. It wraps around an old street light.

The figure leaps off the roof. Bullets ricochet off the ledge.

Terrence pulls the bolt back on his rifle and returns it.

The figure swings down the cable. Cops SCREAM and dive out of the way.

The figure arcs back up and lands on the roof near Terrence.

It's the Penguin!

He drops the rifle and waddles past the Irishman.

                    TERRENCE
               (to himself)
          Jesus, Mary and Saint Joseph.

Terrence quietly climbs down from his spot. He follows the Penguin around a corner. Webbed tracks fade into darkness

                    TERRENCE
          Here birdie, birdie, birdie.

He looks around. Plenty of places here to hide.

                    TERRENCE
          I'm professional, birdie. I promise I'll be
          quick about it.

He pulls a Zippo from his pocket and flicks it. The flag of Ireland is painted on the side. He follows the tracks.

A zeppelin floats overhead, eclipses the moon.

> TERRENCE
> If'n it was up to Mister Hall, he'd have you cooked alive in a pie.

He passes various rooftop structures.

> TERRENCE
> Gotta meet me halfway, birdie. Don't make me go looking for you. The cold's no good for me bones.

The Penguin stands on the roof's edge, his silhouette lit against the sky. Terrence brings the rifle up.

> TERRENCE
> There's a good little birdie.

He squeezes the trigger.

BLAM!

His target shatters into fluffy wet pieces. A snow sculpture of a penguin flies everywhere.

> TERRENCE
> (looking around)
> Wanna play games? Do ya?

Snow and ice CRACK under his feet. He spins around and fires another round--

BLAM!

Another snow sculpture bites the dust.

> TERRENCE
> Playing Terrence for a fool, eh?

The Penguin's head pops out of the darkness, wearing night vision goggles.

INSERT - PENGUIN'S P.O.V.

Terrence walks away, seen though the goggle's grainy green filter. He spins around and fires. The goggles flare up bright as the sun--

                                                            BACK TO:

The Penguin rolls from the darkness and throws his smoking goggles aside.

Terrence pulls back on the rifle bolt.

The Penguin races across the roof with a butterfly knife and gracefully
slashes Terrence's hand.

                         TERRENCE
                    Ya bastard!

He jerks his hand back. The Penguin is gone.

The roof is quiet... Almost too quiet.

The Penguin belly-slides from behind Terrence, slashing his Achille's tendon.
Terrence drops his rifle and falls, SCREAMING.

He reaches for his weapon.

The bird whizzes by and slashes his arm.

                         TERRENCE
                    (screaming)
              I swear to God, I'll kill you, you little shite!

He crawls to the rifle. His fingers brush metal.

The Penguin rushes by and kicks the weapon into the shadows. A blade
FLASHES. Terrence SCREAMS again.

Two severed fingers lay in the snow.

Terrence gets to his knees and clutches his hand.

                         TERRENCE
                    Come out! Come out and fight! Don't
                    hide, you coward!

Yellow eyes with red pupils blink from the shadows. The Penguin waddles
up, Terrence's rifle in his hands.

                         TERRENCE
                    You think I'm afraid of you? You think I'm
                    afraid of dying?

The Penguin steps closer.

                         TERRENCE

Me and Death are close friends. What can
a little bird like you do?

The Penguin SLAMS the butt of the rifle into Terrence's head--

CRACK!

Blackness everywhere...

EXT. ROOF TOP - LATER

Groggy eyes open to a snow-covered roof. The Penguin sits on the roof's
edge, reading a newspaper by the light of a kerosine lantern.

The Penguin meets Terrence's eyes and lets go of the paper. The sheets fly in
the wind like bats in the night.

The Penguin carries the lantern to Terrence. The bartender is naked and tied
to a clothesline frame.

                    TERRENCE
          What'd you do with me clothes?

The Penguin pulls a pack of cigarettes from his 'pocket.' He puts two in his
beak and lights them with Terrence's Zippo.

                    TERRENCE
          Wondered where my lighter was.

The Penguin sticks a cigarette in Terrence's mouth.

                    TERRENCE
          Now what? Think you're gonna get old
          Terrence to talk?

The Penguin shrugs.

                    TERRENCE
          Screw that, little birdie! You might as well
          kill me now.

The Penguin reaches again into his 'pocket.' He pulls out a leather roll and
opens it. Tools of torture GLEAM inside.

Picks. Scaling knives. Hooks and clamps.

Penguin picks up a curved knife. Terrence's eyes grow wide.

                    TERRENCE

It ain't gonna work. Whatever you have
in mind. It's so cold out, I wouldn't feel
anything.

The Penguin pulls out a multi-bladed device. He turns it on. A nozzle spits
fire.

The Penguin looks Terrence in the eye. Then down at his crotch. Terrence's
cigarette falls from his mouth

EXT. COOPER'S APARTMENT BUILDING - CONTINUOUS

Police drag themselves from the building. The sergeant staggers to the
street, pressing a handkerchief to his nose.

                    RED-HEADED SERGEANT
          If I ever find out which of you bastards
          fired first--

A CAPTAIN steps up to the sergeant. The sergeant salutes.

                    POLICE CAPTAIN
               (thick brogue)
          Lot of gunfire up there, Tommy. I expect
          to see some penguin fillet.

                    RED-HEADED SERGEANT
          The penguin wasn't there, Liam--

The Captain shoots him an icy stare.

                    RED-HEADED SERGEANT
          I mean 'Captain.'

                    POLICE CAPTAIN
          All those shots? Sounded like the Easter
          Rebellion up there.

He leans over the sergeant.

                    POLICE CAPTAIN
          I expect a full report on my desk tonight.

                    RED-HEADED SERGEANT
          Yes Captain.

The sergeant salutes captain steps to a waiting police car.

                    POLICE CAPTAIN
               (muttering)

I don't know why I ever let you marry my
sister....

The captain climbs in; the car drives off.

> RED-HEADED SERGEANT
> 'Cause I got the bitch pregnant, that's
> why.

EXT. CANDLETOWN TENEMENT - DAY

Just another neighborhood shit hole.

> CHINNY (V.O.)
> Wee Billy! Where you hiding, fool?

INT. WEE BILLY'S BEDROOM - CONTINUOUS

Wee Billy throws clothes into a suitcase. Chinny storms in.

> CHINNY
> I been looking for--what you doing, man?

> WEE BILLY
> It's called leavin'. I'm leavin'.

He closes the suitcase and drags it past Chinny, out of the room. A shirt
sleeve trails on the floor. Chinny follows.

> CHINNY
> Leaving?

Wee Billy drags his suitcase to the door and drops it next to another one.

Expensive mismatched furniture fills the room. Everything centers around
an enormous radio cabinet.

> WEE BILLY
> Leavin'! That means I'm here now, but I
> ain't here tomorrow. Hell, I ain't gonna be
> here in an hour.

> CHINNY
> What the hell you talking about?

> WEE BILLY
> When we first started, we said we'd do it
> so long it wasn't dangerous.

                    CHINNY
Yeah, so--?

                    WEE BILLY
Well, it's dangerous--

                    CHINNY
It ain't dangerous--

                    WEE BILLY
Knock. Knock... Who's there...? It's
dangerous!

                    CHINNY
Will you isten to yourself?

The two stare at each other.

                    CHINNY
We been together since we was babies.
And now when things start getting good,
you wanna split?

Chinny puts his hands on Wee Billy's shoulder.

                    CHINNY
We always been a team, remember?
Shined shoes together as kids. Worked as
runners for Big Leo before them Italians
shut him down.

                    WEE BILLY
That was messed up, what happened to
him.

                    CHINNY
And when we went to juvie, no one
messed with us. Why? 'Cause we stuck
together!

                    WEE BILLY
I remember when my grandmama saw
me at the center the first time. She--

                    CHINNY
Don't bring your dead grandmama into
my story, man. She ain't in it...
Remember how we helped each other get
out of the Army--?

                    WEE BILLY
          Yeah, by pretending I was slow and you
          was my caretaker.

                    CHINNY
          Yeah. By pretending... Point is, we stuck
          together and stayed outta the war.

Chinny puts his hand on Wee Billy's shoulder.

                    CHINNY
          And when Mister Hall came to me with his
          job offer. I could'a kept it all to myself.
          But I didn't. I wanted you as my partner,
          right?

                    WEE BILLY
          Right--

                    CHINNY
          And you know why?

                    WEE BILLY
          'Cause friends stick together?

                    CHINNY
          'Cause friends stick together!

Chinny points to a sofa.

                    CHINNY
          When you bought that fine leather sofa,
          who helped you carry it up the stairs?

                    WEE BILLY
          You did.

Chinny points to the cabinet stereo.

                    CHINNY
          When you bought your record player,
          who helped you carry it up here?

                    WEE BILLY
          You did.

He points to the Penguin, in the corner, holding a katana.

                    CHINNY

And when you bought that Penguin with
the sword, who helped you--

Chinny and Wee Billy look at each other.

                    CHINNY
          Fuck me...

The Penguin slips toward them, ninja-style.

Wee Billy looks petrified. Chinny's at the end of his rope.

                    CHINNY
               (yells at the Penguin)
          Just what the hell you want?

                    WEE BILLY
          Chinny, don't anger the penguin with the
          sword.

                    CHINNY
          No! This bird's been messin' with us
          since we ran into him on the street!

                    WEE BILLY
          Don't talk crazy, Chinny.

                    CHINNY
          This bird messed my face up! He robbed
          us of our money and product--

                    WEE BILLY
          He did ruin my suit--

                    CHINNY
          What else he gonna do to us?

He SCREAMS in the Penguin's face.

                    CHINNY
          C'mon bird! Show us your worst!

The Penguin sticks his sword in the floor. He pulls something from his
pocket...

And drapes it over his head.

It's Terrence's face!

The Penguin's eyes blink through Terrence's eye holes. His beak peeks
through the mouth.

Chinny and Wee Billy stare in horror.

The Penguin releases a blood-curdling CRY.

Wee Billy and Chinny race to the door. They SLAM into it with a loud THUD and fall comically to the floor.

The Penguin leans over them.

The mask falls off the Penguin. It lands on Chinny's face with a soft SLAP.

EXT. UPSCALE STREET - NIGHT

A serene and beautiful street--ruined by the RING of a telephone.

INT. GREGORY HALL'S BEDROOM - CONTINUOUS

A princess phone RINGS on a night stand. The room is furnished for royalty.

A hand flicks on a Tiffany lamp. A sleepy Hall, in silk pajamas, brings the phone to his ear.

                    HALL
          Hello...? What? How many police?

He sits up in his bed. Silk pajamas cover his doughy frame.

                    HALL
          They found what...? How long ago?

MRS. HALL (50) SNORES in bed. A frilly mask covers her eyes.

                    HALL
          Who let them in my office...? Jesus Christ!

He gets out of bed and steps into slippers.

                    HALL
          Well, call my lawyer. No, not Rubinstein!
          Levitts! Tell him to come over. Right
          away.

He SLAMS the phone down and throws on his robe. His comatose wife doesn't move.

Hall flings open the bedroom door.

CONNELLY, LOUGHLIN and FORD stand at the doorway, dressed in trench coats and fedoras. Connelly's fist is raised to knock a door.

RUTHIE, (65) fidgets behind them, a thin black woman in a modest robe.

                    CONNELLY
          Gregory Hall?

                    HALL
          Yes.

The three flash badges from inside their lapels.

                    CONNELLY
          Clover City Narcotics--

                    LOUGHLIN
          You're coming with us-

                    FORD
          Downtown!

Hall looks at Ruthie.

                    RUTHIE
               (southern drawl)
          I'm sorry Mister Hall. They pushed
          themselves passed me.

                    CONNELLY
          You'll have to deal with staffing problems
          later, Mister Hall--

                    LOUGHLIN
          After you answer a few questions--

                    FORD
          Downtown!

Connelly SLAPS the cuffs on Hall.

INT. POLICE HEADQUARTERS - LATER

REYNOLDS and COYNE (both 40), uniformed cops, drag an Italian-looking
man, CALGIONE (35) through double doors.

SERGEANT O'DOULE (50), sits at the desk and TAPS a pencil on a blotter.

                    O'DOULE
               (brogue)
          What you got here, boys?

REYNOLDS
(brogue)
We found this greaseball behind Royal
Liquors, loading up the back of his car--

CALGIONE
(Italian accent)
Presents for the orphans at Saint
Anthony's.

COYNE
(brogue)
He was filling his car with cases of
whiskey.

O'DOULE
For the orphans?

CALGIONE
I would'a left some for you micks--

O'Doule drops his pencil.

O'DOULE
I dropped my pencil.

He disappears behind the desk to retrieve it. Coyne and Reynolds WHACK
Calgione with their nightsticks.

They stop when O'Doule sits back up.

O'DOULE
Mustn't lose my favorite pencil.

He looks at Calgione, badly beaten.

O'DOULE
Anything else you'd like to say?

CALGIONE
(slurred)
No sir.

O'DOULE
Book him! See what else he's done.

STANLEY LEVITTS (45), an uptight-looking man with thick glasses steps up
to O'Doule.

LEVITTS

Evening, Sergeant.

                    O'DOULE
          Mister Levitts. What brings you out this
          time of night?

Levitts hands him an envelope.

                    LEVITTS
          A letter from the Mayor's office--

EXT. POLICE HEADQUARTERS - LATER

Snow falls, covering the sidewalk and a multitude of sins.

                    LEVITTS (V.O.)
          Demanding the immediate release of one
          of Clover City's most prominent citizens,
          Gregory Hall.

Levitts and Hall walk freely through the front door. Levitts' trench coat
hangs over Hall's robe.

                    HALL
          I'll be meeting with the D.A. first thing in
          the morning.

                    HALL
          I've never been so humiliated in all my
          life.

They step to a limousine. A proper CHAUFFER opens the door.

                    LEVITTS
               (to chauffeur)
          Mister Hall's restaurant. And make it
          quick.

INT. LIMO - CONTINUOUS

Hall looks furious. Levitts seems very much in control.

                    LEVITTS
          My sources tell me the tip came from
          someone known only as 'the Penguin.'

                    HALL
          The Penguin? The bird that's been
          terrorizing our city?

                    LEVITTS
If my sources are to be believed.

                     HALL
A bird isn't a reliable source. I'm
innocent!

                    LEVITTS
The police found twenty pounds of
narcotics in your office. So they say...

                     HALL
The Penguin obviously put it there! He's
wreaking havoc throughout the city. I'm
just another victim of his mad design.

                    LEVITTS
How could a bird plant twenty pounds of
heroin in The Great Hall?

EXT. STREET - CONTINUOUS

The limo cruises down the street.

                   HALL (V.O.)
How would I know? I'm just an innocent
businessman. And a personal friend of
Mayor Johnson.

                  LEVITTS (V.O.)
The police are estimating the street value
at--

                   HALL (V.O.)
I know the street value! Just shut up!

The car disappears in the night.

INT. GREGORY HALL'S OFFICE - MOMENTS LATER

Hall hurries into his office. Levitts follows.

Desk and cabinet drawers are open. Paintings and animal trophies are
pushed aside. The rug is pulled up, revealing a trap door in the floor...
Completely empty.

Hall shakes a fists.

                    LEVITTS
          Anything you need me to do?

                     HALL
          Make sure the charges are dropped. I
          need to be alone for now.

Levitts closes the door behind him. Hall drags himself behind his desk. He looks very old.

CREEEAK....

Hall reaches under his desk, to an empty holster, taped in place.

                     HALL
          I know you're there. Come out. I have a
          gun.

A closet door opens.

                 TERRENCE (O.S.)
               (weak)
          Please don't shoot, Mister Hall...

                     HALL
          Terrence?

Hall walks toward the closet. Terrence is huddled inside.

                     HALL
          What are you doing in there?

He pushes the clothes aside and GASPS.

Terrence is naked. He hides his face in his hands.

                  TERRENCE
          I waited til they left before I snuck in. I'm
          sorry, Mister Hall.

Hall steps back, horrified. The RIPPING of cloth is heard.

                TERRRENCE (O.S.)
          Never seen anything like that bird.

Terrence crawls from the closet. He's all cut up. Dress shirts cover his head and waist.

                     HALL

I'm going to call an ambulance, Terrence.
Get you to the hospital.

He hurries toward his desk and picks up the phone.

                    TERRENCE (O.S.)
          No one ever made me talk before.

Hall gently hangs up.

                    TERRENCE
          Whole time, he stared at me. Smiling.

                    HALL
          This penguin. Where is he?

                    TERRENCE
          I don't know...

Terrence stands and drags himself to a wet bar.

                    TERRENCE
          But I know how to find him. And how to
          lure him out.

He turns to Hall and points to a bottle.

                    TERRENCE
          Could I...?

Hall nods.

Terrence pours a drink with shaky hands and downs it. His makeshift mask
runs red.

                    TERRENCE
          You see, Mister Hall. He has a friend.

                                                  CUT TO:

A WESTERN UNION TELEGRAM. CLOSE UP.

"YOU ARE CORDIALLY INVITED TO PERFORM..."

The Penguin lowers the telegram in his 'hands.' Cooper smiles proudly.

                    COOPER
          They want me to play at the tree lighting
          ceremony?

INT. COOPER'S KITCHEN - CONTINUOUS

Cooper sits in e dark, wearing a coat. The room looks like a bomb hit it.
Sunlight peeks through a broken window.

The Penguin holds the telegram and nods. He wears a candle-powered
miner's helmet.

                    COOPER
          The Clover City Orchestra always plays...
          You don't have anything to do with this,
          do you?

The Penguin shakes his head.

                    COOPER
          Better not find out you did. One of the
          tuba players is a friend.

The Penguins sweeps dirt and plaster into a dust pan.

                    COOPER (V.O.)
          I sometimes wondered about the Penguin.
          Did I come into his life so I can help him?

The bird tosses dirt out the window.

                    COOPER (V.O.)
          Or did he come to help me? If I could get
          him past the holidays, I can show him
          people are good.

The Penguin tosses another pan of dirt out the window.

                    OUTSIDE VOICE (V.O.)
          Hey! Who's throwing shit out the
          window?

The Penguin leaves the kitchen.

                    COOPER (V.O.)
          The way he felt about Christmas, though,
          some things are easier said than done.

The bird waddles back in, carrying the saxophone.

                    COOPER (V.O.)
          And then the solution came to me.

                    COOPER
          You know, bird, maybe I *will* play at the
          lighting. It'll be good. For both of us.

The Penguin smiles.

                    COOPER
          But you gotta promise me something.
          Don't go shooting at no one.

The Penguin looks him for a moment. He nods and CLAPS.

                    COOPER
          Alright, we got a deal.

The bird gives Cooper his sax. Cooper PLAYS soft jazz. The Penguin resumes
sweeping, a huge smile on his face.

EXT. CLOVER CITY PARK ENTRANCE - NIGHT

CAROLLERS in gay apparel sing their hearts into the night as a well-dressed
CROWD gathers by the park entrance. Festive CHATTER is heard.

Police circle the crowd.

Cooper shuffles through the crowd, wearing an old tuxedo, the sax case in
hand.

                    COOPER
          Excuse me... Excuse me... Merry
          Christmas... Excuse me...

The Penguin leads him, wearing an elf-hat and matching tie. He frowns as
people bump into him.

                    COOPER
          You need to see for yourself what the
          spirit of Christmas is about.

The Penguin finds himself face-to-face with a FAT WOMAN's ass. He leans
from side-to-side. He can't get around. She's that friggin huge!

                    COOPER
          Sure it's crowded. Just means everyone's
          having a good time.

The Penguin edges around the woman when--

FFAAAAAAAAARRRRTTTT!!!!!

The Penguin's feathery yellow eyebrows wilt. He changes colors He uses his hat to fan the cloud away.

A nearby MAN glances over. He nudges a WOMAN at his side.

> MAN
> Say, isn't that the Penguin from the
> papers?

The bird quickly puts on the hat as the woman looks down.

> WOMAN
> Newspaper didn't mention anything
> about a hat.

The Penguin leads Cooper away.

They reach police barricades. The Penguin pushes one aside--

> IRISH-LOOKING COP (V.O.)
> Hey! No crossing the line!

Two COPS shove the barricade back.

> COOPER
> Sorry, Officer. My son was just helping
> me get backstage.

> IRISH-LOOKING COP
> Backstage? Really now?

> COOPER
> I'm Benjamin Cooper. I'm playing at the
> Christmas tree lighting.

Cooper pulls out the telegram. The cop looks it over.

> IRISH-LOOKING COP
> I guess you are the entertainment.
> Alright. Hurry up then.

The cops pulls the barricade aside. The Penguin pulls Cooper through.

> 2ND COP
> The short one's his son? Don't see it,
> myself.

> IRISH-LOOKING COP
> Ehh. They all look alike to me.

The Penguin leads Cooper backstage. REBECCA (30), a festively-dressed woman with a clipboard approaches them.

                    REBECCA
          May I help you?

                    COOPER
          Yes ma'am. I'm Benjamin Cooper--

She flips through the clipboard.

                    REBECCA
          Mister Cooper. We have you down as our
          opener, tonight. Are you nervous? All
          these people staring at you when you
          play?

                    COOPER
          I won't be looking at them, ma'am.

                    REBECCA
               (awkward)
          Oh...

                    COOPER
          I hope you don't mind my asking, but who
          hired me? I'd like to thank him,
          personally.

                    REBECCA
          Why, that would be our organizer. And
          here he is now--

She TAPS a tuxedoed man on the back. He turns around--

It's Gregory Hall!

                    REBECCA
          Mister Hall, this is--

                    HALL
          Mister Cooper. It's a pleasure to make
          your acquaintance.

Hall shakes Cooper hand. The bird looks at him suspiciously.

                    HALL
          They say you're an extraordinary
          musician.

                    COOPER
              I'm flattered, Mister Hall.

                    HALL
                (to the Penguin)
          And which of Santa's elves is this?

The Penguin looks disgusted.

                    COOPER
          This is my boy, Benny. He helps me get
          around.

Hall takes off his hat and bows.

                    HALL
          It's a real pleasure to meet you, boy.
          Hope you're excited about tonight.

INSERT - BACK STAGE - THROUGH CROSSHAIRS

Hall waves his hat about the Penguin dramatically.

                    TERRENCE (V.O.)
              There you go, little birdie--

                                                    BACK TO:

INTERCUT - STAGE/TELEPHONE POLE - CONTINUOUS

A masked Terrence hides in the shadows, strapped to the top of the pole. A
rifle rests in his hands

                    TERRENCE
          Your disguise may fool some people, but
          not Ol' Terrence.

Hall puts his hat back on.

Terrence peeks through the rifle scope. The Penguin is dead center in the
cross-hairs.

He squeezes the trigger...

A FIGURE steps in front of the Penguin, blocking him from Terrence's view.

                    TERRENCE (V.O.)
              What the-?

Hall and Cooper continue talking.

                    HALL
          --Looking exceedingly forward to tonight.

MAYOR JOHNSON (40) steps up. A dapper man in a tux.

                    JOHNSON
          Gregory, shall we begin?

Johnson blocks Terrence's view once again.

                    TERRENCE (O.S.)
          Move over, you stupid bastard. You're
          blocking my shot.

THROUGH THE CROSS-HAIRS

Johnson and Hall walk away, leaving Cooper alone.

The Penguin is gone!

                    TERRENCE (O.S.)
          Hey--

The scope swings around and scans the crowd.

                    TERRENCE (O.S.)
          Where'd the birdie go?

Cooper screws the mouthpiece in his sax

                    COOPER
          Gonna to be a special night for both of us,
          Bird. My big break in Clover City. Your
          chance to experience the Christmas spirit-
          -

He turns from side to side, looks concerned.

                    COOPER
          You with me, Bird...?

Rebecca taps Cooper on the shoulder.

                    REBECCA
          Mister Cooper, we're ready.

                    COOPER
          Now? Have you seen my boy?

                         REBECCA
                   We'll find him for you--

She grabs his sleeve and leads him away.

                       JOHNSON (V.O.)
                         (amplified)
                   Merry Christmas, Clover City.

The crowd erupts in APPLAUSE. SPECTATORS hang on to the mayor's every
word.

Rebecca leads Cooper past the manger scene.

                       JOHNSON (V.O.)
                   Clover City has a very special Christmas
                   this year--

The Penguin perches atop the manger, dressed like an angel. His anxious
eyes dart around.

Johnson stands in front of the unlit tree and speaks into a microphone.

                         JOHNSON
                   Santa Claus has brought our family back
                   to us. The war is over!

The crowd APPLAUDS. Johnson smiles.

INT. DEERBORN TAVERN - CONTINUOUS

Gunner sits at the bar, in his Army jacket. He stares at the radio, beer in
hand.

                       JOHNSON (V.O.)
                         (static)
                   It's time for Clover City to celebrate the
                   return of its heroes. Man and woman.
                   White and black.

Georgina SNORES, collapsed on the bar.

APPLAUSE ripples through radio static.

Georgina's dentures fall from her mouth.

SILENT NIGHT plays over the radio, the song of a single saxophone.

                                                         BACK TO:

THE STAGE

Cooper stands on stage, the tree at his back.

The crowd falls silent. PARENTS hug their KIDS. LOVERS kiss and hold hands.

The Penguin listens from his perch. For once, he's at peace.

Cooper changes the tempo and adds a jazzy beat.

Mayor Johnson SNAPS his fingers to the music. Hall glares at him, annoyed.

Cooper swings around the stage, in his jazzman ballet. The audience loves him.

Cross hairs sweep the area. No Penguin in sight!

                    TERRENCE (O.S.)
          Where are you, little birdie? Terrence
          ain't got all night.

Cross hairs scan the Nativity scene. Terrence's view of the 'Penguin-Angel' is blocked by a string of lights.

The Penguin remains on his perch.

Cooper dances toward the back of the stage. He swings a leg out and accidentally kicks a low hanging branch.

Several balls fall from the tree, hit the stage with a POP! POP! POP--!

--It sounds like gunfire!

Terrence swings toward Cooper--

BLAM!

The bullet hits Cooper in the leg. He SCREAMS and crumples to the floor.

The crowd GASPS.

The Penguin leaps from his perch. Draws a double-barrel derringer as he lands.

He strips off his costume as he rolls across the stage.

                    WOMAN IN CROWD
               (screams)
          It's the Angel of Death!

The woman faints. SCREAMS are heard.

COPS struggle to reach the stage. They're forced back by the panicked crowd.

The Penguin fires twice at Terrence.

KPOW! KPOW!

One shot cuts Terrence's harness straps. He drops a foot. Jerks to a stop. He swings and fires another round.

It hits the stage inches from Cooper.

The Penguin reloads.

                    COOPER
          No! Don't kill anyone! Please

Terrence reloads as well.

The Penguin rushes to Cooper, shielding him.

                    COOPER
          It's Christmas! You promised me, Bird!

Terrence fires and hits Cooper in the leg again. He SCREAMS!

The Penguin shoots back... hits Terrence twice. The Irishman hangs limply from the pole.

Cops rush the stage, guns drawn.

Hall stands off stage, enjoying the show.

The cops surround the bird, revolvers drawn.

                    IRISH SARGEANT
          Alright men, get him! Now

The Penguin looks at Cooper and quickly rolls him off the stage, into the tree.

The Penguin somersaults across the stage... a rain of gunfire in his wake.

He bounces off Hall's chest. Bullets hit the restaurateur in the gut. He falls like a ton of well-dressed bricks.

The Penguin stops to reload when--

BLAM!

He looks down. Blood oozes from his chest.

The bird falls to the stage. Blood pools at his webbed feet.

                    IRISH SARGEANT
          We got him, men! We got the Penguin!

The cops CHEER wildly and slap each other on the back.

                    COOPER (O.S.)
          Nooooo!

Cooper crawls along the stage. His glasses are missing, exposing lifeless eyes.

                    COOPER
          Stop cheering! He didn't deserve this!

Cooper feels around the stage and finds the Penguin. He cradles him in his arms and cries.

                    COOPER
          He was my friend and you killed him. All
          of you!

The Penguin opens his eyes and GROANS.

                    COOPER
          You're alive? We'll get you to a doctor,
          Bird. Get you fixed up--

                    COOPER (V.O.)
          "It's too late for me," he said... "But
          thanks for lying, anyway."

The crowd falls quiet, watching the scene.

                    COOPER (V.O.)
          He told me, "Lying is comforting, when
          the truth isn't."

Several COPS remove their hats in respect.

The Penguin pulls out two blood-stained envelopes from a breast pocket and lays them in Cooper's hand.

                    COOPER (V.O.)
          "Merry Christmas, Cooper..."

                    COOPER
          A Christmas present? I didn't get you
          anything, Bird?

The Penguin talks slowly (MOS).

                    COOPER
          "You did. Friendship," he told me... And a
          little peace of mind."

Two cops step toward Cooper. They try taking the Penguin. Cooper pulls the
bird to his chest and hugs him.

                    COOPER
          No! Don't touch him! You got no right!

The cops jump back. MURMURS of discontent spread through the crowd.

                    SPECTATOR (V.O.)
          They shot a sweet little penguin--

                    SPECTATOR 2 (V.O.)
          --It's just a bird--

                    SPECTATOR 3 (V.O.)
          --He was protecting that blind musician--

                    YOUNG SPECTATOR (V.O.)
          --Mommy, I'm scared.

Cooper cries and rocks the Penguin in his arms.

                    COOPER (V.O.)
          The Penguin died in my arms that night.
          Despite how it happened, he died in
          peace...

The crowd gathers around them.

                    COOPER (V.O.)
          Knowing that he had a friend.

EXT. CLOVER PARK ENTRANCE - DAY

The Christmas tree is brightly lit. KIDS play in the snow.

                    COOPER (V.O.)
          Wasn't too long before most people forgot
          that night.

KIDS build snowmen. One sculpture has a Penguin shape.

                    COOPER (V.O.)

> Almost everyone... But those envelopes
> the Penguin gave me contained some
> special papers.

EXT. HIGHWAY - DAY

A CHAIN GANG digs ditches along a road. Chinny and Wee Billy work with them in prison stripes.

> COOPER (V.O.)
> The first had signed statements from
> Chinny and Wee Billy, swearing that
> Gregory Hall supplied them with drugs.

Chinny stops digging and turns to Wee Billy.

> CHINNY
> Man, this work is killing me.

> WEE BILLY
> I know what you mean. But, as my
> grandmama use to say, "When you put
> your back into your work--"

> CHINNY
> Wee Billy, the last thing I wanna hear
> about is your dead grandmama.

Wee Billy raises his shovel and--

KLANG!!!

Knocks Chinny out.

EXT. CLOVER CITY PENITENTIARY - DAY

A gothic block of concrete despair. GUARDS patrol the yards with SNARLING DOGS.

> COOPER (V.O.)
> Gregory Hall was convicted for his
> crimes--

INT. PENITENTIARY MESS HALL - CONTINUOUS

Scores of CONVICTS stand in line with trays in their hands. A ladle slops gruel onto a tray. Grey gravy splashes on a slice of bread.

COOPER (V.O.)
And sentenced to the Clover Penitentiary
for eighty years.

Hall looks at the meal, disgust on his whiskered face.

EXT. CLOVER CITY HOSPITAL - DAY

An ambulance arrives. PEOPLE walk in and out the main door.

COOPER (V.O.)
As for me, well, the Penguin left me a
couple of special things in that other
envelope...

INT. HOSPITAL CORRIDOR - CONTINUOUS

NURSES push PATIENTS in wheelchairs.

COOPER (V.O.)
Savings accounts in four of Clover City's
banks, totalling.... Well, more money than
I care to talk about.

INT. PATIENT'S ROOM - CONTINUOUS

A DOCTOR and two NURSES stand at a patient's bed.

COOPER (V.O.)
He also left me something else... His eyes.
I didn't know it but Penguin eye balls are
completely compatible with people eyes.

The doctor unwraps gauze from the patient's face. A thin black man.

COOPER (V.O.)
Knowing he was going to die, he gave me
his. Gave a poor musician the gift of sight.

The bandages are removed, revealing Cooper. Small pads of cotton are taped
over his eyes.

COOPER (V.O.)
Like all Christmas stories, there is a
moral. Though not everyone may realize
it.

The doctor reaches for the cotton.

                    COOPER (V.O.)
          It might be that you can always find good
          in everyone.

Cooper opens YELLOW EYES with BLACK PUPILS. He looks around the room,
amazed.

                    COOPER (V.O.)
          Or that good will always triumph over
          evil.

The doctor talks to Cooper (MOS). Cooper glances back and nods.

                    COOPER (V.O.)
          Or it might just be--

Cooper turns directly to the camera and grins. His pupils turn red; his
eyebrows arch.

                    COOPER (V.O.)
          Don't fuck with the Bad Penguin!

                                        FINAL FADE
                                        OUT